Copyright © 2024 by KC Hart

To my amazing friend and sister in Christ, Lisa Turley. You are an inspiration.

KC Hart

Our Unfailing Love

Red Creek Redemption Book 2

Also by KC Hart

Our Head Strong Love

A Christmas Blaze

Fresh Starts and Small Town Hearts

Business Smarts and Reckless Hearts

Car Smarts and Bashful Hearts

People Smarts and Wounded Hearts

Kid Smarts and Wistful Hearts

Family Smarts and Runaway Hearts

Elsie: Prairie Roses Collection

Moonlight, Murder and Small Town Secrets

Music, Murder and Small Town Romance

Memories, Murder and Small Town Money

Merry Murder and Small Town Santas

Medicine Murder and Small Town Scandal

Marriage, Murder & Small Town Schemes

Mistaken Murder & Small Town Status

Mistletoe, Murder & Small Town Scoundrels

Join KC's newsletter and receive a free ebook of Music Smarts and
Humble Hearts

If you enjoy my books, please consider leaving a review where you purchased them.

Chapter One

Friday afternoon, Oscar wedged his finger into the knot at the base of his throat and yanked on his tie. He slammed his truck door shut and continued to loosen the silk noose around his neck, taking long strides toward his house as he did so. The duplex, sunny yellow with white trim, the place where he had lived for the past eight months, where he kept his stuff and slept, was not his home. His home burned down at the end of last summer, nearly taking the life of his father.

For a while, a couple of months actually, he'd stayed with Odi, one of his four brothers. Three lived in Red Creek, and the other, Ori, had moved to Nashville. Odi lived in an apartment near where they both worked, and he'd been fine with Oscar staying there until he found a place of his own. Oscar was on the Creek bank camping and fishing every weekend, and they both worked through the week, so they didn't really have time to get in each other's way. Oscar was a big guy, over six-foot-tall with linebacker shoulders. Even though he didn't have any trouble getting comfortable on the ground in his sleeping bag every Friday and Saturday night, trying to bed down on Odi's couch during the week had proven to be nearly impossible. Plus, he had missed his dog. His parents had let the animal stay with them without giving it a second thought, but Festus was his responsibility and his friend.

Oscar slipped the key in the lock and opened his front door, tossing the red silk tie on the wing-back chair that came with the house, and his black suit coat on the back of the color coordinated sofa. He hated having to keep the door locked and forgot to do it half the time. This wasn't supposed to be a prison, it was supposed to be a home. They never locked their doors when he lived in the family home place outside of town. "Festus?" Oscar listened as canine toenails tapped against the ceramic tile floor in the kitchen. A couple of seconds later, an enormous golden lab bounded across the room at full speed and jumped up onto Oscar's chest, his long pink tongue slathering Oscar's five o'clock shadow in drool.

Oscar shoved the dog's mouth away from his face and scratched the animal's neck. "You about ready to head out, boy?" The dog continued to prop up on Oscar's chest while he petted his silky butter-colored coat a while longer. In truth, Festus had taken to their new place better than Oscar. The dog door in the kitchen led to a fenced in back yard he shared with the other half of the duplex. Thankfully, that half had remained unoccupied so far, giving Festus the run of the yard. If someone ever rented the adjoining living quarters, he sure hoped they liked dogs . . . big dogs that liked to slobber and dig holes.

Thirty minutes later, Oscar set a loaded down ice chest in the back of his vehicle. He opened the truck door, and Festus jumped in and circled a couple of times before sitting in his usual seat on the passenger's side. Oscar slid behind the wheel, his faded blue jeans, Alabama Crimson Tide t-shirt, and worn cowboy boots a far cry from how he'd exited his vehicle less than an hour before. He backed out of the driveway and headed down the quiet road.

A moving van passed him going in the opposite direction, and Festus let out a soft woof. Over the past year, more and more people were moving into Red Creek. This was a good thing. Grow or die seemed to be the way of the world, but change didn't excite Oscar like it did his brother Ori. Ori packed up and moved to Nashville not long after their parents reunited and renewed their vows last year. Having a mother in their life after growing up with only their father would definitely be change enough for Oscar.

Oscar sighed. The strange house, or half a house he now rented, was not part of the plan. Set a course, reach your goals, or die trying. Running through life on a wing and prayer more often than not led to problems. Ori didn't seem to mind heading off willy-nilly into the unknown, and that was fine. Let Ori do Ori. Oscar had a plan, and he was working it.

His truck continued out of town, houses and trailers dotting the landscape between small sections of overgrown forest. A field full of black cattle scattered behind a barbed wire fence stretching along the blacktop road appeared to his right. He slowed his truck and turned in on the gravel side road. Several of the cattle still had the tags on their ears where Aunt Sadie had purchased them at the sale barn last week. She was too old to be raising cattle, but she was too hardheaded to listen to reason.

Aunt Sadie was a workaholic. That's why they got along so well. She didn't have children of her own, and now that Oscar and his five siblings were grown, she needed something to occupy her time. Before Momma came back into the picture, his aunt always stepped in to help their father do pretty much whatever was needed. Now though . . . well, maybe she did need those cows.

Oscar didn't begrudge his parents their rekindled love, or

whatever they called it. His dad looked happier than he ever remembered seeing him. His mother—it still felt a little weird calling Lucy Robinson momma—even though she had given birth to him. It almost felt disrespectful to Aunt Sadie.

He bumped along the rut-filled road, cluttered with little potholes from the recent rain. The cattle casually lifted their heads to watch him as the truck passed. Festus let out an energetic bark, and Oscar let the passenger side window down so the dog could hang out his head. He passed by Aunt Sadie's wood-framed house and waved to the gray-headed woman talking to somebody in a white double-cab pickup. Who was that? What was his aunt up to now?

He slowed the truck as he passed Aunt Sadie's house and turned on an even more narrow gravel road that was little more than a path. He crept along, lowering his window and breathing in the wonderful smell of the woods and the flowing water of Red Creek. The river had been cutting a path through this land way longer than the Robinson's had.

Last year, after the Robinson home burned, his father had built a new place. Even though Oscar's newly reacquainted mother had said Oscar could live with them, his father said no. Not that Oscar wanted to anyway. Living with his single parent at the age of thirty-two was one thing. He and two of his siblings had lived in the old home place with their father, helping him take care of the place. Now that their mother was back in the picture, and they had built a new house of their own together, it didn't seem right being there. It wasn't right.

He glanced at the mixture of pin oaks, water oaks, pine trees, and cedars all growing together on either side of his truck, making a canopy across the make-shift road. The sun peaked through the cool evening shade and streaked the gravel and packed down earth ahead with slivers of yellow light. A blue jay flew across the front of his windshield. He wasn't lonely. That wasn't the word to describe him.

Oscar wanted to be a bachelor, and he definitely didn't want kids. Orville Robinson had dedicated his entire life to raising Oscar, his brothers, and one baby sister. The man didn't seem to regret it at all. Oscar had seen the sacrifices his father made. His father had basically given up his life for his kids, not that he had once complained, but Oscar wasn't his father. No, he just had to adjust the plan a little, keep working, moving up in the business, saving the money, build the house . . . and what?

Oscar eased his truck under a water oak in the clearing a few yards from the creek. Right here, Red Creek was larger than it was behind his father's place, more like a river. The ice-cold rushing water, the occasional call of a blue jay, or bark of a squirrel all made the tension from the past week at work ease from his shoulders. This place, this piece of land that his father deeded him last year when he tried to buy it, was his sanctuary. It was his escape from all the demands, the conflicts, the unrealistic expectations heaped on him at the office.

He put the truck in park, and Festus stepped over the console, pushing his eighty-pound body into Oscar's lap so he could lean his head and shoulders out the window. "Alright, boy. You are my boy, aren't you?" Festus pulled his head back in the window. Oscar let the dog lick his cheek for a couples of seconds, enjoying the affection. He weaved his hand under the dog's furry chest and opened the truck door, setting the animal free to explore the woods and all the treasures of frogs, rabbits, squirrels, and anything else his overly energetic pet could chase and sniff.

Oscar climbed out of the truck and walked over to his tent, the one he set up a couple of months ago after the first one blew away in a particularly nasty thunderstorm. Everything was still anchored down, and there were no surprise visitors of the slithering variety hidden inside. He walked to the creek bank and checked out his boat sitting on the rocky shoreline. He would fish all day tomorrow, spend the night under the stars, then run into town for morning church, and fish all of Sunday afternoon. By then, he'd be ready to tackle whatever the big announcement was that his bosses, the Crestfield brothers, were going to unleash on Monday. A new client was what he guessed, with the flow of vacationers coming through town. Somebody wanted to build a gas station or another restaurant or some sort of tourist trap. They probably needed to have Oscar at the meeting to make sure everything ran smoothly, and that was fine. It was part of his job, after all.

The Crestfield brothers owned the accounting firm, but over the past ten years, they had become less and less involved in the day-to-day operation of things. Oscar took care of all their major clients, and the brothers popped in from time to time to make sure things were running as they should. The two men would take Gordon Blue, their biggest account holder, or the bank president out to lunch, then disappear for another week or two. If Oscar took an extended vacation, not that this was going to happen, the accounting and investment business would be on hold until he came back.

Oscar checked the trolling motor on the back of his fishing boat, then turned and walked toward the woods to gather a few limbs for a fire. Festus met him on the other side of the truck, rubbing against his leg and wiggling like he hadn't seen him in days. Oscar reached down and picked up a limb about the length of his forearm as he petted the happy-go-lucky dog again.

This. This was all he needed to be content, his dog, his land, and Red Creek to fish in. He looked at the sun, dipping toward the west, ending another day. He rolled his head on his shoulders and bent down to pick up a few more sticks. Crickets started chirping in the distance. A lightning bug flashed a few feet away in the dimming twilight. One of Aunt

Sadie's cows mooed from her field on the other side of the woods. The steady ripple of Red Creek continued in the backdrop, always there, always constant. Daddy and Momma finding each other and falling in love again after all these years was good—for them, but Oscar was not like them. Not at all.

Chapter Two

Fifer McKenzie pulled her sleek red Miata into the short, paved parking spot and looked at the canary yellow, two-story duplex complete with a tiny porch and a navy blue rocking chair. She inspected the front of her new home for the next six months to a year. It wasn't as bad as she feared coming to a place named Red Creek in the state of Alabama. Well, she had to admit, she had a few preconceived ideas about what she'd gotten herself into. It wasn't the "Big Apple," but it wasn't *Little House On The Prairie* either. Not exactly. When she'd turned off the interstate, just past the enormous Blue Hotel that the richest man in Alabama owned, she was delayed for several minutes by an unusual sight. A guy in blue jean overalls, muddy boots, and nothing else loaded an enormous black pig into the back of his truck which he had left parked in the middle of the road. The pig had a huge set of dingy yellow tusks protruding from under its snout. She'd never seen anything like it except for when she went to the zoo as a child and saw the fat walrus flopped out on the side of the pool waiting to be fed. The pig's tusks turned up instead of down like the walrus's tusks had. Plus, she'd never seen a pig with such a thick black coat of fur, but truthfully, she'd seen very few pigs in her life at all. This was fine with her. The top to the Miata was down, and she hadn't smelled anything piggy. Didn't those animals stink?

On second thought, this wasn't like *Little House On The Prairie*. It did, however, resemble an episode or two of *Green Acres* and P*etticoat Junction* she'd seen while visiting her grandmother as a child. Fifer opened the car's little door. She dabbed a bead of perspiration from her neck and strode across the patch of green grass. She pulled the house key from her black leather bag and slipped it into the door lock. Two men with arms like tree trunks began bringing in her boxes from the moving van parked on the curb and piling them on the floor. A painting of a cow's face, its thick lashes and innocent brown eyes stared at her from its place of honor over the white mantle above the fireplace across the room. She rolled her eyes. *Just call me Zsa Zsa. Wasn't that the name of the city lady from Green Acres?*

She stepped around a stack of cardboard boxes over to the fireplace, her black heels clicking on the hardwood floor. Her slender arms, well-toned from afternoon sessions of yoga done religiously to keep her body and mind in perfect control, lifted the picture down and turned. "Take this with you when you go." She held out the bovine on canvas to the mover. He dropped another load of boxes and looked at Fifer, his brow pulling low.

"Ma'am?"

"This." She stuck the canvas out further in his direction, the white of her French manicured nails blending well with the blue sky behind the animal's face. "Take this cow picture."

"Take it where, ma'am?" The man reached out and accepted the picture, still frowning.

"I don't care. To the dump, to your mother, back to the tasteless store it came from. It doesn't matter to me." Her top teeth, even whiter than her manicured fingertips, bit down on her lower lip as her eyes scanned the room. "As a matter of fact, let me do a walk through before you leave. I have a feeling there's a few more things that need to leave here. Immediately."

"But, ma'am, we can't just take . . ."

"Stop calling me ma'am, and yes you can." Fifer walked into the kitchen, not bothering to look back at the man in the gray coveralls. "I'm going to need a box," she called over her shoulder. "A large box."

She picked up a foot-tall figurine of two pigs from the granite countertop, one in overalls and the other in an apron, and turned. The mover stepped through the kitchen door and dropped the cardboard box on the floor, disappearing again before she could give him any more orders. She put the figurine in the box along with several pictures of various sizes of smiling, happy livestock that adorned the walls. The chicken salt and pepper shakers were the last things she dropped into the box. She looked at the curtains, white with a baby blue checked ruffle along the edges. They had to come down, but she would tackle that later.

Her heels clicked back through the living room, quickly filling up with boxes. She walked over to the staircase and looked back at the second mover, a bodybuilder type with a shaved, tanned head. "Grab that box out of the kitchen, and do not leave until I get whatever else needs to go from up here."

"Yes, ma'am."

Fifer's lips turned down, and she hurried up the stairs, collecting several more pieces of farmhouse décor that had to leave before she would be able to sleep in this place. Her heels clicked as she walked back down the stairs ten minutes later, stepping carefully with arms full of pictures, throw pillows, and a few more figurines. She unloaded the items into the first mover's arms. "Is there a place around here to get halfway decent sushi?"

The loaded down mover's brow lowered once more, and he looked at his partner sporting the Mr. Clean persona. "Lady." Mr. Clean's lips turned up in a slight grin. "The only place you're gonna find raw fish around these parts is down on Red Creek. I don't see you as the fishing type, though."

Monday morning, Fifer pulled her car into the parking lot behind the office building where she would spend the majority of her life for at least the next six months. She had circled the block, checking the place out. At least the front of the building looked nice-ish. The brick building stood flush with the sidewalk, the olive-green awning covering the oak door, and the plate glass window beside it were charming in a southern sort of way. It fit the idea out of towners would look for when they drove through Red Creek on their way to the coast. Crestfield Brothers Financial Advisors painted across the middle of the window in an easy to read, but tasteful font, gave the place a certain sense of old school charm.

Fifer looked around as she killed her engine. The back of the building needed a facelift, even if the people who worked in the rows of offices and businesses beside Crestfield Brothers were probably the only ones using this lot for parking. If Red Creek was going to draw in the tourists like the mayor and town council wanted, little details, like rundown parking areas, had to be addressed.

Fifer pushed down a yawn and reached over to get her

briefcase from the floorboard. Since moving in late Friday evening, she'd done nothing but unload boxes and put things away. She usually got up early to do morning yoga, but making a thousand trips up and down the stairs, lifting and carrying and putting away her things, had made her too tired to follow her usual routine. That was not good, but after today, things would get back on track. She would make sure of that.

Sleep had come easily so far, but a truck pulling in Sunday night after she was in bed awakened her. It must have been her neighbor, and he apparently had a dog. A barking dog. She planned to introduce herself after work this afternoon and lay down a few ground rules.

A pewter colored truck pulled into the parking spot two spaces down from hers, and she watched as a man climbed from the cab. His coal black hair was short, but a curl still kicked up across his forehead. He looked her way and smiled, his blue eyes fringed with lashes as dark as his hair. She smiled and nodded her head. It was nice to see a man in something besides overalls, coveralls, or worn-out clothes in general. She lowered her eyes and pretended to look in the briefcase resting in her lap, waiting to see which building he entered. The man disappeared into the Crestfield office, and she pulled in a deep breath. Coming in the back door meant he worked there, and from his clothing, he probably was one of the owners. She'd never actually met the Crestfield brothers since her father set up this venture. She'd assumed the men were her father's age, but apparently, she was wrong, at least about one of them.

Fifer stepped out of her little car and headed inside. Her slim black skirt, white silk blouse, and black jacket made her look smart, professional, and in charge. She made sure of that. Her red hair with the unruly curls she inherited from her Scottish grandmother, along with the odd name, required a bit more work to produce the image of success she insisted on presenting. Over the years, though, she had become an expert at slicking the mass of fiery red ringlets into a no-nonsense chignon at the base of her neck. They would stay put with a few minor tweaks until she set them free that afternoon.

Fifer moved from the bright morning sunlight into the dim lighting of the back hall leading toward the front offices of the Crestfield building. At least she assumed that's where it led. "Oh." She blinked again, bumping into something, actually someone in front of her. "Excuse me. I didn't see you."

The man turned around and looked down at Fifer, an unusual occurrence. Fifer was five foot ten and wearing her two-inch heels. "No harm done."

The man's deep voice fit with his broad shoulders and square jaw. His bright blue eyes looked at Fifer as heat eased up her neck. *What in the world? He's an Alabama redneck and definitely not your type, Fifer, even if he is nice looking.* "Excuse me again." She stepped around the man and walked on, forcing each step to be slow and controlled. She should have introduced herself. If this man was her boss, she needed to show him she was confident and in control.

She walked into the front lobby, and the secretary directed her through a door and into a small conference room where two men, both at least in their sixties, sat. They stood in unison and smiled. "Good morning." One man stepped forward and stuck out his hand. "I'm Bill Crestfield and this is my baby brother, Grant. You must be Fifer McKenzie."

"I am." Fifer shook Bill's hand and then Grant's. If these were the owners, who was the man in the hall? "I'm looking forward to working with you, gentlemen. I have a lot of great ideas for the building you purchased that I think will work well with the tourists who will come through your area."

"Take a seat." Bill nodded toward one of the vacant leather chairs as he sat and straightened his silver tie. "Oscar should be here any second, and we can get started."

"Oscar?"

"Yes." Bill's face pasted on a business-like smile. "Oscar is who will be working with you. He and Grant handle all the day to day hands-on decisions for our business." He looked at Grant, who smiled briefly at Fifer, then looked away. "I scout out new investment opportunities and discover ways to turn the investments into a profit. Grant and Oscar take the projects and run with them after that."

"I see." Fifer set the briefcase in the chair beside hers. So, she wouldn't be working directly with the owners. That could be a good thing. Without Bill breathing down her neck and micromanaging every decision, she might get this job done and be out of this town in less than six months. If Oscar was as timid as Grant seemed to be, she was going to have smooth sailing.

"Ah, Oscar." Bill stood again with Grant right behind him, like his silent shadow. "Meet Fifer McKenzie. Her father is Louis McKenzie. She's going to be renovating the old movie theater for us."

Did they have to tell him they knew her father? Fifer stood and forced a smile. Great. the man who would be working under her was also the hot guy from the parking lot—the man who saw her blushing like a school girl just a few minutes ago. Well, at least he wasn't going to be her boss. "It's a pleasure to actually meet you, Oscar."

"You too, Fifer. I thought you were going to be a guy."

Chapter Three

Oscar watched the woman's face, her jaw clenching at his words. "I'm sorry. That was probably rude of me." He smiled, taking in the fiery red hair, a rebellious curl escaping from the tight knot at the base of the woman's neck. The curl hung softly against her pale cheek. Was her skin as soft as it looked? "What kind of name is Fifer, anyway?"

"Fifer is Scottish." The woman's slender hand reached up and tucked the wayward curl back into the bun. "I was named after my grandmother."

"It's ahh . . ." Oscar's blue eyes held firm as Fifer's green eyes dared him to look away. *She's spunky. That's for sure.*

Fifer's left eyebrow raised. "A beautiful name?"

"I was thinking an unusual name." His lips turned up at the corners. He reached down and picked up the leather briefcase in the seat next to her. "But beautiful works, too. May I have this seat, Miss McKenzie?"

"Of course." Fifer took her briefcase from him and put it on the other side of her chair, looking away and breaking their eye contact.

Oscar slid into the chair next to the attractive woman, his eyes following her movements, but stopping on the nice set of legs extending from her snug skirt. The skirt lacked quite a bit of material needed to make the ensemble hit her knees.

"Are you done?"

Oscar lifted his head and looked again at Fifer's one lifted eyebrow, her lips drawn into a thin line. "Excuse me?" Yes, he'd been staring at her legs. No, he would not admit it.

"If you are done ogling me," she said, "I think everyone is ready to start."

Oscar grinned. "Seems to me that when a person puts their wares on display, they want them to be noticed. I was just . . . noticing."

"Are you serious?" Green daggers shot from Fifer's eyes. "I'll have you know that this is a designer suit and probably costs more money than you make in a week."

Oscar's grin broadened. He leaned back in his chair and tucked his chin, his eyes trailing back down to her legs. "I'd say it was worth every penny, too."

"Well." Bill Crestfield cleared his throat and tapped a folder on the table. "As Miss McKenzie said, we, um, should get started."

Oscar sat up straight in his chair, not looking over at the woman beside him. His boss began explaining about the building he had recently purchased and what he expected to happen with it. Oscar focused his eyes across the table on Bill Crestfield as his mind wandered. What had come over him? He was not rude to women, and he certainly didn't need to get on this particular woman's bad side. She was nice looking, that was true, but he was not the type of man that, what? What had he been doing a few seconds ago? He didn't leer at women —even if they were wearing a skirt that was meant for someone about three inches shorter. Aunt Sadie would pinch his ear if she saw him acting like that. Of course, Aunt Sadie would never have let his little sister Olivia dress that way either.

That was neither here nor there. The important thing was, he had to get along with this woman. He didn't want her to think she would be working for a crude sexist pig. No, he would apologize after the meeting and try to start over.

"Oscar?" Bill Crestfield's voice broke through Oscar's self-dialog. "Is that okay with you?"

"I'm sorry." Oscar cleared his throat. "Would you mind repeating that?"

"I said, why don't you two start out by going to the old theater and let Miss McKenzie see the place? She can give you some ideas about the renovation, and you can come up with a cost analysis." The older man looked from Oscar to Fifer. "Oscar's family has lived here for generations. My brother and I want you to modernize the building, but we need you to make sure that it keeps the essence of Red Creek. Oscar can help you with knowing if your ideas will, uh, mesh with the feel of the rest of our little town."

"Yes, sir. That will be fine." Oscar glanced over at Fifer. "That is, if Miss McKenzie agrees."

"Of course." Fifer looked down and picked a non-existent piece if fuzz from her jacket. "Whatever it takes to get the job done. Be assured, Mr. Crestfield. I will do my part to make this work."

Yeah. He'd ticked her off, and now he was going to pay. He looked at her stubborn chin. What did he expect from a woman with hair the color of fire? The Crestfields pushed their chairs away from the table and stood. "Don't worry," Oscar said. He stood, shaking first Grant's hand, then Bill's. "We are going to turn this building into something you will be proud to have the Crestfield name on."

The older men shook Fifer's hand, then left the two of

them standing alone in the room. Oscar turned and watched Fifer slip her folder into her briefcase. "Miss McKenzie . . ."

"Fifer."

"Fifer." Oscar watched her close the briefcase. She took her dear sweet time, probably enjoying making him wait. He needed to be able to work with this woman. Rushing her and ordering her around would not sit well with her.

Finally, she lifted her head and looked at him. "Go on."

"I'm sorry we got off on the wrong foot. I'm not the type of man that . . . ." He frowned.

"Ogles. I believe that's the word you are looking for."

"Okay." Oscar raked his fingers across his jaw. "I'm not the type of man that ogles a woman. You have the right to wear your skirt as short . . ." Fifer's eyes narrowed, and Oscar winced. "You have the right to wear whatever you please, the same as anyone else does. I don't have the right to be—"

"Obnoxious."

"I was going to say rude." Oscar pulled in a breath of air. She was making this hard, and she knew it. "What I'm trying to say is, it won't happen again. You don't have to worry about working with me. I can, and will be a perfect gentleman."

"Good." Fifer pulled the briefcase from the table and stepped toward the door. "I will meet you at the theater at two." She opened the door and looked over her shoulder. "Oscar, don't think for a minute that because you look like you look, and I'm a woman, that you can get away with anything. I will treat you with dignity and respect. I expect the same from you."

"Of course." Oscar nodded. "That goes without saying."

"Good." Fifer stepped through the door and turned. "I can be a great boss or a terrible boss. The choice is up to you."

Oscar's brow wrinkled as he looked at the door slowly swinging shut. Boss? Wait. She's not my . . . "You're not my boss, lady."

Fifer opened the front door to her side of the duplex. She slipped off her black pumps and padded across the cool hardwood floors to the adjoining kitchen. From what Bill Crestfield had said in the meeting, and from the notes he had given them, the theater she was going to see was in a pretty sad shape of disrepair. The power had not been turned back on yet, but she would get her new assistant to take care of that.

She opened her stainless-steel refrigerator door and pulled out a Styrofoam box of leftovers she'd picked up from the restaurant inside the Blue Hotel yesterday afternoon. She needed to find a grocery store and see what eating places delivered around here. That would be another thing she could get her assistant to do, make a list of places like that. He also needed to get her a map of the town. She rubbed her hand across the tight muscles in her neck. She definitely had to get back into her routine. The tension was building inside her, pulling at her insides. It had to get out before it made her slip.

She pulled one of the red Fiesta ware plates from the cabinet and transferred the rest of the salmon and steamed vegetables onto it, then put it in the microwave. At least the place had a furnished kitchen. She grabbed a glass and filled it with ice, then water from the refrigerator door. Things had not gone great with her assistant, Oscar. Had his parents watched Sesame Street and named him after that puppet from the trash can? It sure seemed to fit. She looked down at her skirt, then dropped her hand down her side, her fingertips grazing the hem of the black fabric. In high school, the dress code, and not to mention her father's code, had been, all skirts must be at least fingertip length. The microwave beeped, and she stepped over and pulled out her plate. "If it's good enough for Principal Davis and Father, it better be good enough for you, Oscar Robinson."

She ate her food quickly, wishing she had a little more of the cornbread and chocolate cake that had come with the meal. Both of those had been devoured last night. She put her dishes in the sink and turned as a bump sounded against the back door. She walked over and looked out the window at the top of the door, but no one was there. The door bumped again, and she cracked it open. A cold black nose pushed through the crack and touched her lower thigh.

"Well, hello there." Fifer opened the door further, and a beautiful yellow dog pushed his way inside. He trotted around the island bar, pausing to sniff her barstools and cabinets, then returned and looked up, nudging his head against her leg. "Are you the one who woke me up the other night?" She squatted down and petted the dog, who returned the affection with a lick to her cheek. "I forgive you this time, but . . . ." She pushed his thick yellow fur away from his collar. "Festus? You don't seem like a Festus. I think I'll call you John." The dog licked her again. "Okay. John it is. Anyway, John. You are going to have to keep you voice down in the evening when I'm trying to sleep."

The dog let out a soft woof, and Fifer laughed. "I think you and I will get along fine." She looked up at the clock hanging on the nearby cream-colored wall. "I've got to hurry, boy. It's time for you to go." She opened the back door, but the dog turned and strolled through the kitchen. Fifer shut the door. "John! Come here!" She stepped into the compact living room. No dog. A playful woof sounded at the top of the stairs. "Alright. You can hang out with me for a little while, but I've got to change and hit the road, mister."

Fifer grabbed her heels, still waiting by the front door,

then climbed the stairs. A lapping sound came from the nearby bathroom, and she wrinkled her nose. "John, gentlemen do not drink from toilets." She grabbed the dog's collar and drug him from the bathroom and closed the door behind her. "Let me change, and I'll get you some water—in a real bowl."

Fifer removed her skirt and other office attire and slipped on her favorite pair of boyfriend jeans and a green pullover sweater. She pushed her feet into a pair of canvas sneakers and looked at the dog, flopped out across her bed like he belonged there. "Come on, boy. I can see right now that Oscar Robinson is not the only male I've met today that's going to require a little training on how to treat a lady."

Fifer persuaded the dog back down the stairs. She pulled a tiny piece a salmon left over from lunch and tossed it into the backyard. The dog took the bait and ran out of the kitchen. She quickly shut the door behind him. Yes. She definitely had to talk to her neighbor about some boundaries. She loved dogs, but she couldn't have anyone or anything pushing in on her personal space.

Chapter Four

O scar pulled his pickup in front of the old run-
down movie theater and looked at his watch. The
boss lady would be pulling up any minute. After
she left him standing in the meeting room like a slack-jawed
monkey, he decided he needed to clear up a few details. He'd
assumed he was running this project. Before, he was the one
put in charge of any large endeavors the brothers dreamed up.
It stood to reason that this project wouldn't be any different.
Then again, this project was different. This would be the first
time for the brothers to go into a project all on their own
without a board of investors having input. It was also the first
time they'd ever shown any interest in anything related to
tourism or hospitality.

Yeah, times were changing around Red Creek. The Crestfield brothers were great at picking projects with a money-
making potential. Oscar looked at the old building through his
windshield. He'd passed the place thousands of times through
the years, but had never paid it much attention. The brick
building, its tall cathedral-like storefront wrapping around the
corner, with the marque sign extending out in front over the

rounded ticket booth below, held a sort of sad grandeur. Silver duct tape covered cracks in the glass doors on either side of the ticket booth, and the entire structure reminded him of an era that had disappeared long before he was born.

He looked over as Fifer pulled her cartoonish, little red convertible sports car into the parking space beside him. She'd changed clothes. He looked down at his suit pants and white dress shirt. Oh well, too late now. He'd spent the time after their meeting trying to confirm exactly what his role was in this venture, and where he stood in the pecking order with Fifer McKenzie. After that, he'd looked into digging up a little history on the building. Neither venture had made him eager for this meeting. She was running the project, but he was still supposed to carry out his duties like he always did, and report back to the brothers. Oscar climbed out of his truck and walked up to the rundown building where Fifer was already waiting.

"Do you have the key?" Fifer cupped her hands around her face and looked through the grimy glass door. "I'll need you to contact the power company and get some electricity flowing to this place."

"I did that about an hour ago." Oscar stepped closer to Fifer and slipped the key into the lock, then pulled open the door. Stale air met his nose. He held up a maglight in his other hand. "I only brought one flashlight."

"I can use the light on my phone." Fifer pulled her cell phone from the back pocket of her jeans. "We won't be able to tell much today other than how the place feels."

Oscar held the door open and followed her through, clicking on the light in his hand. The aroma of dust and abandoned dreams overwhelmed his senses as the beam from his light hit the lobby. "It feels like it needs a good cleaning and a whole lot of work." The beam of light roamed around the room, taking in the vaulted ceiling, the scuffed and scarred wood floor, the counter on the back wall piled high with old cardboard boxes. Broken cinema chairs, part of a commode, a beauty shop chair with a ripped seat, an ancient vending machine laying on its side, and a hodgepodge of other junk was scattered around the room. "Lots of work."

Fifer shined her phone light, making a path through the maze of other people's forgotten belongings. She weaved between a box of Styrofoam mannequin heads and a crate of VHS tapes, making her way to the counter. "Are you coming?" She shined the light back in Oscar's direction. "Or do you want me to yell at you across the room? We are going to need to find out who owns all this junk. We'll have to contact them to come get their junk. We'll have to make it clear that if they don't remove their belongings after a certain amount of time, we will take the stuff to the dump."

"The Crestfields own the building and all the contents." Oscar moved toward the counter, weaving a different path. A box of movie posters caught his eye. He squatted down to look at Princess Leah and Luke Skywalker, running his fingers along the edges of the memorabilia from the seventies. "I know a guy that will come clear all this stuff out for us." *Dad will be like a kid in a candy store going through all this junk.*

"Shop around and get someone who will work cheap." Fifer's voice floated from somewhere behind the boxes stacked on the counter. "We can't waste money on these sorts of things."

"Yes, ma'am." Oscar stood up and rolled his eyes. Did she really think he didn't know anything? "I have a connection with the local junk guy. He is going to be the cheapest person around. He'll probably do it for free if you let him have all this stuff."

"No water." Fifer reappeared around the edge of the counter. "You need to call the water department and have it turned back on. Add that to your list." She reached up and rubbed the tip of her nose, then sneezed. "Electricity, water, junk removal and cleaning. Got it?"

Oscar clicked his heels together and saluted. "Aye, aye, general."

Fifer turned her back to Oscar and looked at the double doors off to the side of the counter, not acknowledging his actions. "Find something to prop open the theater door. It's going to be completely dark back there, but we need to at least try looking around."

She doesn't need a partner or an assistant. She needs a trained monkey. Oscar's long legs stepped over the side of the vending machine blocking his path and followed her to the double doors covered in grimy maroon velvet. He looked around and picked up a five-gallon bucket of coal patch. "Hold the door open."

"What's that?" Fifer pointed to the bucket as she pulled the door open and pushed it back against the wall behind them. Dust flurries filled the air.

Oscar set the bucket in front of the door and waited while she sneezed again. "You put it on leaky roofs." Her lips turned down, and she raised her finger to speak, but paused for the second sneeze that followed. "I know," he said. "Get the roof checked. I'll put it on my list. I have the number of a building contractor that I want to give us an overall estimate on what needs to be done."

Truth be told, he had already called the man and left a message to schedule a walk-through of the building to get a ballpark estimate. He had planned on going through the place with his new partner, then heading back to the office, and discussing renovations and other needs with her then. Her style seemed to be more of a, 'Fifer snaps her fingers and Oscar jumps through the hoop,' sort of thing. He'd let her do that . . . for now, long enough to see how competent she would be at this job. After that, some changes were coming.

⌘

Fifer stepped through the doorway of the theater lobby into the pitch-black auditorium, the smell of closed in dampness and dust falling over her like a cloak. She looked back over her shoulder to Oscar standing in the dim light coming through the distant filthy windows at the front of the lobby. A shuffling noise from somewhere in the distance above their heads sent a shiver down her backbone. "Good thinking." Her eyes darted to the yellowed ceiling tiles above their heads. "Add a pest control inspection to that list as well."

"Okay." Oscar raised the flashlight and shined it over her head, panning the cavernous room around them. The aisle sloped gently forward toward the screen area on the other side.

"Where are all the chairs?" Fifer looked at the gutted room. The beam of light found more boxes and piles of debris, stacks of folding chairs and tables, along with a few couches that looked like they'd been around since the seventies. "This looks more like a storage shed than a theater room."

"The building has been bought and resold several times. It hasn't been used as a movie theater in decades." He stepped beside her and Fifer moved further into the room. "When I was a kid, one of the churches rented this place out while they were building their new facility. I can't remember anything being in here in years, though."

"What's that?" Fifer's phone light shone down in front of her and she weaved her way toward a black metal box with a rounded top sitting over to the side near an enormous pile of old cloth. Her eyes narrowed as they adjusted to the darkness, taking in the box large enough for a full-grown person to lie in. She looked back to Oscar, still standing near the doorway, shining his flashlight this way and that. "Come here. I need your light." She turned back to the box, slipped her phone in her front pocket, blinking against the momentary darkness. The light behind her flittered around, bouncing off the different objects in Oscar's path. Fifer felt along the lid of the box and lifted as a long creek echoed through the room. "What in the world?" She pushed the lid up and pulled her phone out of her pocket, aiming her light at the contents of the box.

A scream filled her lungs as her mind took in the skeletal face, the empty eye sockets staring back at her. A coffin? A dead body? Her heart pounded in her ears as the shrill of her own voice echoed in her head. Her phone fell from her hands and she turned, her legs trying to move her away from whatever it was she had uncovered. What kind of town had she moved to?

"Hey, hey, hey." Oscar's calming voice surrounded her. Her screaming stopped, but her pounding heart filled her ears. Warm arms pulled her in, steadying her as her legs gave way beneath. She took in a deep breath and blew it out, forcing her body to do what she wanted it to.

"There's a . . ." She swallowed and cleared her throat, pushing her head and shoulders off of Oscar's chest where they had landed in her panic to get away from what she had seen. "There's a dead . . . a body in that box."

"A body?" The flashlight left Fifer's face and focused on the now open box behind them.

"Yes." Fifer's eyes stretched wide, the disbelief in Oscar's voice stiffening her spine. "Go see for yourself. There's a body in that box." She turned and pointed. "I know what I saw."

Oscar stepped past her, and Fifer turned, holding on to the back of his shirt. There was no way in the world he was leaving her standing in this creepy place in the dark. She felt his torso dip down, then come back up. "You dropped this," he said, the light from her cell phone shining between them.

"Thank you." She took the phone and pointed it toward the box. "Is that some kind of weird coffin? What in the world happened here?"

Oscar stepped up to the box and chuckled. "You're right." He reached in and picked up the skeleton, the black wig on its head sticking out it all directions. "I forgot all about this."

"About what?" Was this man bonkers? What kind of person forgot there was a coffin and a body stashed in an abandoned movie theater? A psycho, that's what kind. Her calves hit the material, and she stumbled. Fifer stepped backwards, her legs bumping into the pile of material piled at the end of the metal coffin. Her arms shot out, grabbing for anything to break her fall, her legs slipping on the discarded junk at her feet.

Oscar's arms reached out for the second time, saving her from hitting the ground. "Don't freak out, Fifer." He dropped the pile of bones, attired in a flowered dress that looked like it belonged on somebody's great grandma, back in its coffin. "This isn't a murder scene. Back when I was a teen, they used this place as a haunted house. At Halloween, the people that owned it at the time would fix the place up and sell tickets to walk through it. One of my little brothers volunteered as a zombie."

Fifer stepped away from the pile of material and smoothed down her shirt. Oscar released her arms from his grasp. She eased up to the box, taking a closer look at what was now obviously a plastic skeleton. "What is this thing it's in?" She leaned forward, shining her light on the interior of the box.

"It's an old tanning bed." Oscar pointed to the bulbs lining the inside of the box lid. "They painted it black. The first year they did this, Joyce Cooley laid in this thing and raised the lid when people walked by." He laughed and pushed the lid closed. "They had to start using the skeleton after the first night. When she leaned forward with her fake fangs and pasty make-up, Cletus Wells almost snatched her bald. He jerked her so hard she fell out of the coffin and cracked her tail-bone on the floor."

Fifer looked at Oscar, no words coming to her brain to respond to a story like that. "Okay. Well." She shined her light around the rest of the room. "I think I'm done here." She started back toward the lobby. "Oh. By the way, I need you to get me a map of the town and make a list of where I can buy groceries, get my nails done, and any places that will deliver food. But no fast food, only real food. I'd like that on my desk by the end of the day, please."

Chapter Five

"Hey, Oscar. I thought that was you." Fifer turned from where Oscar was locking the door of the theater and looked at the ancient truck pulled up next to their vehicles. A man that could have been Oscar's twin, except older with a touch of grey in his black hair, looked out the truck window. "Your momma made chicken and dumplings for supper. Reckon you can come?"

"Yes, sir." Oscar turned and looked at Orville Robinson, a picture of how he would look in twenty years—minus the worn-out pickup. "That sounds good. Around five?"

"Better make it six." Orville leaned his head further out the window of the rusty old truck. "You're welcome to come too, ma'am. Lucy fixed a pot big enough to feed half of Red Creek."

Fifer looked from the man, half shouting across the parking lot in their direction, to Oscar. "Someone you know?"

"My father." Oscar dropped the theater keys in Fifer's outstretched hand. "Dad, this is Fifer McKenzie. She's working for the Crestfields now."

"Hello, Fiver McKenzie," Orville called, his lips turning up in a smile. "I'm Orville. Nice to meet you."

Fifer looked from Oscar, still standing in front of the theater door, then back to the man several feet away. He didn't seem to be leaving anytime soon. She dusted her hands together trying to wipe away the layer of the grime she'd accumulated over the last hour picking her way through the run-down building, then started walking toward the truck. If she was going to talk to the man, she wasn't going to yell.

"Where are you going?" Oscar stepped up beside her.

"To talk to your father. He doesn't seem to be leaving any time soon, and I am not going to shout at him."

"I appreciate the invitation, Mr. Robinson, but . . ."

Orville extended his hand out the truck window to Fifer. "Just call me Orville."

"Orville." Fifer took the man's hand and shook it. "I'm afraid I am busy this evening."

"Well, maybe next time." Orville tilted his head toward the theater. "What are you going to do with the old movie house? Not tear it down, I hope."

"No, sir. The plan is to renovate it and make it into something useful for the community." Fifer followed Orville's gaze to the dilapidated building. "It's in horrible shape, but I'm certain we can save the original floors, the molding, and some other things. It has good bones." She looked back at Orville and smiled. "Hopefully, we will bring it back to its former glory."

"Wouldn't that be something?" Orville looked at Oscar. "I used to go to the movies there when I was a kid. I even took Lucy there a few times, too, when we were dating. I'm not sure I'd want to see any of the stuff they put on the screen nowadays, though."

"We're not going to make it into another movie theater, Dad," Oscar said.

"What are you going to do with it?" Orville pulled his arm back in the truck window. "Once the theater shut down, that building's been everything from a make-shift church to a beauty shop."

"We are planning . . ."

Fifer cut off Oscar before he could finish. "We are still in the planning phase, but it won't be a beauty shop. I'm certain of that." She reached up and tucked a red curl behind her ear that had escaped from her bun. "I don't see it being a church either."

"Good." Orville adjusted his body behind the steering wheel. "We have plenty of both of those. Nice meeting you, Fiver."

"It's actually Fifer." Fifer stepped away from the truck as Orville put it in gear. "I'm named after my grandmother. It's Scottish."

"I was thinking being named after a five-dollar bill was sort of odd." Orville winked at Fifer. "You're a lot prettier than Abraham Lincoln." He grinned and looked at Oscar. "See you tonight, son. Goodbye, Fifer. Hope to see you again soon."

"Your father is nice." Fifer watched the old truck ease onto the street and disappear from sight. The poor old man. His truck was falling apart, and he was probably as poor as a mouse, but it didn't seem to bother him. She looked at her sports car and over at Oscar's nice truck. Did Oscar help support his father? Was he a good son? She couldn't ask him, of course. That would be rude. Plus, she didn't know this man from Adam. She needed to keep things simple between the two of them so she could do her job. His relationship with his father was his business, just like her and Louis McKenzie's relationship was hers.

"Hmph." Oscar opened his truck door. "You should have seen him last year—or pretty much any time before my mother came back. Nice was not on his radar."

"Came back?"

"Never mind." Oscar slid into his truck seat. "I've got an errand to run, then I'm heading back to the office. Do you remember how to get there?"

"Of course." Fifer slipped her hand into the front of her jeans pocket and pulled out her car key. "This town only has a few streets, and I have a good sense of direction."

"Good. I'll see you there."

Fifer watched Oscar's truck pull onto the road and speed away in the opposite direction that his father had gone. She got in her car and pulled up her GPS, scanning over the instructions to drive to the Crestfield offices.

Her phone buzzed, and she looked at her father's face on the screen. Her stomach tightened into a knot and she hit ignore. No, Oscar Robinson didn't have a clue. There was no way Orville Robinson could hold a candle to Louis McKenzie when it came to obnoxious fathers. Hers had that market cornered, and whether she liked it or not, she was here for one real purpose. To do his dirty work.

She started her car and looked down at the directions to the office. No, she couldn't afford to be nice to these people. That would make doing what she had to do even harder, and she had to do what her father wanted. The stakes were too high for her to rebel against him.

Oscar hung up his phone and leaned back in his chair. After leaving the theater, he'd run by the only pest control office in town to schedule a visit to the run-down building. Harold, the guy who owned the company, said his son had checked the place for termite damage back when it was inspected before the Crestfields bought the place. There wasn't any wood damage then, which was a good thing, but rodents were another matter.

Oscar hadn't said anything to Fifer, but he'd seen several signs of something, probably mice, living in the old building. The woman had not reacted well to the plastic skeleton. If she'd guessed there were rats running loose around the place, she probably would have freaked out. Of course, that old tanning bed did look pretty weird painted black, especially with a bag of bones laying in there wearing an old dress and a frazzled wig.

Her weak moment, where she allowed herself to fall onto his chest, had only lasted a few seconds, before her iron wall had returned. For just those few seconds, she had leaned on him, let him hold her up. He sat up straight in his chair and rolled his head around on his shoulders. She had been soft, and she smelled good too. He was clueless about flowers or perfume. Growing up without a mother in the house, having four younger brothers and only one sister, he didn't have a clue how women made themselves seem so . . . different, so nice. He'd dated a couple of times in high school, but he had been a pimple-faced kid back then. In college, going to school on a football scholarship, his life had been consumed with practice, games, making the grades, and holding down a part-time job. Unlike a lot of his friends whose parents were paying for their education, getting his degree was a one-shot deal. If he blew it, he would pay for it for the rest of his life.

Even so, he'd been out with a few girls. Had they smelled as good as the bossy woman he'd held for a few seconds this afternoon? If they had, he didn't remember it.

"Oscar?" Grant Crestfield, the quiet brother, stuck his head in the door of Oscar's office. "How did things go this afternoon?"

"The place needs a lot of work." Oscar watched the man step in and shut the door behind him. "Have a seat, sir."

"Thank you." Grant Crestfield eased into the leather chair on the other side of Oscar's desk. "It does, that's true." He rubbed his lips together, and Oscar waited patiently for the man to speak. "I've only been over there once, and that was the day Bill decided we needed to buy it. Of course, I remember going there as a boy, but you get what I mean."

"Yes, sir." Oscar stared at his boss. "Did you not agree with the purchase, Mr. Crestfield?"

"Oh, no." Grant Crestfield rubbed his jaw. "Nothing like that. It's just that you and me, Oscar, we're numbers men. We deal with facts and figures. Absolutes. I guess I am having a harder time visualizing what Bill is seeing in the place." His eyes narrowed, then he looked at Oscar. "Is our little town ready for a dinner theater? Bill keeps reminding me that in the past two years, Gordon Blue has made a killing with that new hotel he built on the edge of town. Your sister also opened up her restaurant last year, and it seems to be doing well."

"Yes, sir. It is." Oscar nodded. "Especially since she was featured in *Southern Cuisine Magazine* in December."

"So." Grant pulled in a deep breath. "You believe this is a sound investment?"

Oscar reached down and straightened a stack of papers on his desk, then sat back in his chair. It was not unusual for Grant Crestfield to come to him when he had doubts about his brother's investments. Oscar was always honest with his opinions, but he also had to be careful with how he phrased things. Bill Crestfield was, after all, his boss and Grant's older brother. "Our town is changing. We are definitely seeing an influx of traffic coming through Red Creek, and a lot of these people are tourists. They all have to eat."

"That's true." Bill nodded. "And this woman, Fifer McKenzie. What do you think about her? Does she seem to know what she's doing? You two didn't seem to get off on the right foot this morning."

"No." Oscar's eyes once again looked away. "That's true." He looked back at Grant who was watching him. "Part of that was my fault, and it won't happen again. We were only together for a short time this afternoon, but she appears to be very competent. She asked me to get a contractor to come look at the place, find out if we own the contents of the building so we can get the place cleaned up, have the roof checked . . . all the standard procedures."

"I thought you had already started doing some of those things."

"I have." Oscar shrugged his shoulders. "But we haven't had a chance to sit down and talk about everything, so she didn't know that." Oscar's brow lowered. "Sir, while we're on the subject of Fifer McKenzie, I need to ask a couple of questions."

"Okay." Grant Crestfield shifted his hips in his chair. "Do we need to call in Bill? He was on the phone with Louis McKenzie a minute ago, but he's probably off by now."

"No. That's not necessary." Oscar pulled in a slow breath. Might as well take the bull by the horns. "The thing is this. She thinks she's my boss, that I'm her personal assistant or something like that. She told me to do all the things I said—which is fine—but she also told me to get her a map of the town and make a list of places for her to buy groceries and things like that. I understand we are working together, and she is overseeing everything, but how far does this overseeing go? Exactly?"

"Well . . ." Grant drug the word out slowly. "You don't want to do those things for her?"

"It's not that I mind getting this information for her." Oscar frowned. He sounded like a school kid tattling on the teacher's pet. "Red Creek is not that big. I can make the list in about half a minute."

"But you don't want to." Grant raised his eyebrows, confusion showing on his face.

"I." Oscar blew out a puff of air. "You know what? I'm being petty. Forget what I said. I'll get the lists for Fifer today. I guess I want to clear up if she and I are working together or if I'm working for her."

"You're not really working for her. You work for Bill and I, just like you always have." Grant pushed his lips together. "But her father is very important to us, Oscar. I'm not asking you to bow to her whims, but if you could," he paused. "If you could get along with her, it would make all of this go a whole lot smoother."

Chapter Six

Fifer's phone buzzed as she pulled her car into the paved drive in front of the attractive little duplex. She looked at the face of her father on the cell screen and sighed. That's how he had made his millions. He refused to be ignored and would pursue whatever he wanted relentlessly until he got results. Right now, he wanted to talk to her and wouldn't stop calling until she answered. "Hello Father."

"I spoke to Crestfield this afternoon. He said you're a hardnose. Sounds like you are making progress already."

Fifer opened her car door and reached into the back seat for her bag of groceries. "Did he actually call me that?" She hefted the groceries into her arms and bumped the car door closed with her hip. "I can't imagine that polite southern gentleman insulting me in that way."

"No. But that's what he meant." Her father's laugh was not pleasant. "He said something like, you were holding your own with their best man. I think you may have intimidated the old guy and his brother a little bit. That's good. Make sure they understand who's in charge."

Fifer walked up the short drive and set the grocery bag in the rocker beside the front door. "Oh, they all think I'm bossy. Don't worry."

"Good. Don't forget, Fifer. You're there to get this business going the way I want it to go. That's the only thing you need to focus on. Do that and you have nothing to worry about. Get off course and . . ."

Her father left the threat hanging in the air. "I understand, Father." She switched her phone to her other ear and fished her house key from her purse. "Is there anything else you need? I'm sort of busy."

"Just one thing. When I call you, answer your phone. I shouldn't have to tell you this." Louis McKenzie's voice hardened. How was this man her father? He treated her more like a commodity that he had very little use for, not like his own flesh and blood. "If you don't answer, text me with a good reason why. I will not be ignored or put off, Fifer. Especially not by you."

"Goodbye, Father." The phone disconnected, and Fifer dropped it in her purse. She opened the door, grabbed her groceries, and hurried inside. How had she gotten into this mess? The craving, one that was always there in the distance, tried to rise inside her. Her father usually had that effect on her, but not with this intensity. After the scare with the skeleton this morning, and not doing her yoga over the weekend, the need was a lot louder in her brain. She swallowed and hurried to the kitchen. She'd planned on cooking, then getting this house in order, but all of that would have to wait. She hurried upstairs and changed into yoga pants and a tank top. She popped in a set of ear buds, grabbed her mat, and rushed downstairs. The only way to get the craving out of her was to work it out. Past experience had taught her that ignoring the early signs only made it harder to refocus later. She spread her mat on the hardwood floor, turned on the classical cello music in her ear buds, and took a deep breath. The past was still controlling her. Her father's tentacles held her securely in his web, but she would not—could not let him rattle her. She was strong. She had overcome the cravings before. She would not go down that path again.

Breathe in, control the breath, control the movement, breathe out. She moved from one pose to the next, focusing on her body, leaning into each stretch, letting the tension release, and the music wash it away. Forty-five minutes later, her body sweaty, her mind clear, her thoughts once again under control, she rolled up her mat and pulled the buds from her ears.

A vehicle pulled into the drive next door, and she listened as she opened her refrigerator and pulled out what she needed. Mushrooms, onions, skirt steak, bell pepper, tortillas, an avocado, and a lime. She would season and sauté everything, wrap it up in a warm tortilla with some homemade guacamole and a tiny dab of sour cream, her go to meal when she'd had a trying day.

The front door in the adjoining home opened and closed. A minute later, the back door opened, and the dog's familiar bark sounded. She smiled at the trouble she'd had coaxing the animal out of her house earlier. Thank goodness she'd had that bite of salmon left on her plate. At the time, there was nothing else in the house to eat. It's not that she minded having the dog around. It was the idea of things being—not the way she was used to. She needed things done the way she wanted them done. The way she could handle them. The dog was not hers, and she shouldn't have to worry about it coming into her home.

A few minutes later, the wonderful aroma of her make-shift fajita filled her kitchen as she assembled the hot food on her plate. She sat at her island bar and took a bite, ignoring the bumping at her backdoor. John, or Festus, obviously smelled the food as well. She would have to talk to her neighbor. She liked the dog, but some ground rules had to be laid down. She couldn't have the animal trying to come into her house every time she went to her kitchen, and she needed access to her own backyard. One of the reasons she had leased this place was because of the backyard. She enjoyed exercising outside but needed privacy to focus. She would not be able to focus with the friendly dog running around, licking her in the face . . . sniffing.

There was always music at the Robinson house now. Lucy Robinson, Oscar's mother, had come back into his family's life and brought the music with her. Unlike his father, mother, and his brother Orl, who seemed to need the music to fully express themselves, Oscar had not known it was missing until it returned. His father had quit playing any of the instruments he kept in their home when their mother moved away when Oscar was only eight.

Back then, none of the kids even knew their father could play—or sing—or write songs. Now, every time they got together, Orville pulled out his new fiddle or his old guitar or the mandolin or harmonica or dulcimer and serenaded them with a tune or twelve.

Orville's collection of instruments was growing. Tonight, he showed them an accordion he'd bought at an estate sale. "I can't play it yet, but give me time," he said, looking at the strange instrument lying beside him on the front porch swing.

"I'm going to play, and your momma is going to learn to yodel. We might even go on the road together."

"I can already yodel, thank you very much." Lucy Robinson moved the instrument and sat on the swing beside her husband. "And we aren't going anywhere, and you know it."

Everybody at the house knew it. Oscar's father was just as much of a homebody as Oscar, maybe more. All the kids minus Ori, who was now living in Nashville, had been at their parent's house tonight, just like they were every Sunday after church. Olivia's husband and baby, and Aunt Sadie were there as well, filling the house with family.

Oscar smiled softly. His big, loud, crazy family was all he needed to make him feel complete. And Festus, of course. He unbuckled his seatbelt and reached behind the truck seat to get the container of chicken and dumplings Momma had sent home with him. They were good, probably as good as Aunt Sadie's, but he wouldn't tell is momma that.

"Hold on, boy." Oscar clipped the leash to the dog's collar before opening his truck door. Festus ran free at his father's place. The dog loved wandering into the nearby cow fields between the Robinson home and Aunt Sadie's place, or going into the woods behind the house and harassing the squirrels. Here in town, if Oscar didn't attach the leash, the dog would dart away, expecting the same freedom in town as he had in the country.

Oscar opened his truck door, and Festus jumped from his lap, where he had wedged himself two seconds earlier. "Slow down before you jerk my arm off." Oscar reached in his truck for the dumplings, then shut the door, the dog tugging him along. "Well, that's about right." The dog pulled at the leash, straining to get to the tires of the familiar car in the driveway next door that Oscar had not noticed when he drove up. "Nope. You are not whizzing on the lady's tires." Oscar drug the dog toward the front porch. "The last thing I need is for my new partner to have a reason to complain about me. She'd probably expect me to take her little toy car and get it washed while she stayed at the office in her short skirt looking all . . ."

Oscar opened his front door and shut it behind him. He reached down and unhooked the leash, not finishing the thought. Festus disappeared out of the living room, and his toenails briefly clicked on the kitchen tile before everything was quiet again. Oscar hung the leash on the hook by the door and followed the animal through the house. The dog door swayed gently, and the faint whiff of Mexican food, good smelling Mexican food, tickled Oscar's nose. Where had she gotten Mexican food? There wasn't a Mexican restaurant in town. Olivia's place didn't serve it, but maybe the restaurant at the Blue Hotel did. He'd only eaten there once or twice at a lunch meeting with one of the Crestfield clients. He always ordered their burger, but if the Mexican dish tasted as good as it smelled, he would have to give it a try next time.

He put his bowl of dumplings in the fridge as a knock sounded on his back door. "Hello, Fifer." Oscar's eyes glanced up and down Fifer's toned curves, taking in her neck, a fiery red curl sticking to the damp skin, then stopping on her face with its normal authoritative glare in place. "Would you like to come in? I have some leftover chicken and dumplings my mother made, but it smells like you've already eaten."

Fifer bumped against the door frame as Festus bulldozed his way past her and back into the house. "I'm fine, thank you. I was just returning your dog." She tilted her head toward Festus, who settled into a sitting position at Oscar's feet. "He came and introduced himself earlier today and was back again a few seconds ago."

"Yeah." Oscar reached down and scratched his lab's ears. "He's a pretty friendly fella. Don't worry about him. He won't bite, and he's friendly with other dogs if you have one."

"No. I don't have a dog."

"Are you sure you don't want to come in?" Oscar straightened. "I have tea in the fridge and Coke and water."

"No."

Fifer bit her lower lip, and Oscar smiled. She was kind of cute when she wasn't acting like a drill sergeant. "I guess I'll see you at work tomorrow then."

"About your dog." The look of supreme overlord that Oscar was used to returned to Fifer's face. "He entered my house uninvited this afternoon and bumps on my backdoor every time I go into my kitchen to eat. I plan on using the backyard, and I see he also has free rein there. I don't want this to be a problem between us, but I must insist that you control him better."

Festus stepped over and rubbed against Fifer's leg, golden hair sticking to her black yoga pants. "Come here, Festus." Oscar reached down and grabbed the dog's collar, pulling him further into the kitchen. "You understand that the backyard is . . ." Oscar paused, Grant's words reverberating in his head. He had to get along with this domineering woman. Grant hadn't said as much, but implied that this whole business deal depended on keeping this woman happy, which would keep her rich father happy. "We'll do better. I'm sorry he bothered you. It won't happen again."

The corners of Fifer's lips turned down. She looked at the dog, then back at Oscar. "Thank you." Her voice was soft, the edge gone. "Good evening."

"Good evening." Oscar watched her walk away and listened as her door opened and closed. He shut his door and looked down at Festus. "Sorry, boy." He stepped over to the folding doors on the nearby wall and opened them. A roll of duct tape lay above the washer and dryer that fit perfectly in the enclosed alcove. He picked it up and returned to the back door, Festus making every step with him. "She won't be here long, I imagine, then you can have free rein again."

Oscar taped the dog entrance closed, then nudged it with his hand. "That should do it." The dog sniffed the tape, then looked up at Oscar and whined. "I know. They say I'm her partner, but for right now, she's the boss, whether we like it or not."

Chapter Seven

"We have to figure out what the tourists will find entertaining, will turn a profit for the owners, and will reflect the mood of the area while respecting its persona as well." Fifer looked at the slides on the laptop between her and Oscar. "I worked on this last night to give you some ideas about what works well at other dinner theaters."

Oscar looked at the picture of Dolly's Stampede. "That's in Missouri? We can't bring horses or hogs into the theater here."

"No, of course not." Fifer pushed several strands of red curls back from her face. She had overslept this morning and hadn't taken the time to put her hair up for work. After talking with Oscar about his dog last night, she had gone home feeling more like a thug than a neighbor. Father would have been proud. She'd cleaned her kitchen, drowned herself in work, making this slideshow, then went to bed, and stared at the ceiling. She replayed what she'd said to Oscar last night, how she'd expected him to respond, to tell her to mind her own business. That half the yard was his, and if she didn't like it, she could move. She had expected that and could handle that, but that didn't happen. He'd acted like he wanted to say something, but instead he'd been . . . nice. He'd been nice, and she'd been a bully.

Being a bully at work was one thing. She had to push and shove into the business world to get anything accomplished. At least that's the way it was done in the world she was expected to function in, but did she really want to be a bully in the other parts of her life?

"Fifer?"

Oscar's voice broke through her thoughts. She blinked and turned from staring at the doorway where the Crestfield brothers had entered. "What did you say?" She looked over at Oscar, sitting a couple of feet away at the conference table. His face held an expression of something—what? He wasn't smirking at her like he had the last time they were in here. He didn't look angry. *He's studying me.*

"I said I've never been to the Dolly Stampede. You'll have to explain how you want to make this work in Red Creek in our little theater."

"I don't want to copy the Dolly Stampede." She flipped through the next couple of slides, showing different parts of the show. "It is an enormous operation. There's one in Missouri and another in Tennessee, but that doesn't mean it would play well here in Alabama, even if we did have the budget and the space to put it on."

"Which we don't." Bill Crestfield stepped around the table and stood behind Fifer and Oscar, followed by Grant. They both looked at the pictures. "I've seen it a couple of times over the years, and our operating budget wouldn't even buy all the food it takes to prepare the meal for one of Dolly's shows."

"That's what I was thinking." Oscar's brow pulled down.

"I'm afraid you'll have to come up with something else on a smaller scale."

Fifer caught herself before she rolled her eyes. She pushed her lips into a smile and turned to the men. "That's not why I'm showing you these slides. I know we can't put on a show like this." She clicked the mouse to the next picture of a Pirate themed show put on at an amusement park in California. "What I'm trying to do is give you an overall idea of what we are going for. This is the Swashbucklers." She clicked again. "Here's a Sherlock Holmes style mystery show." Click. "And this is a wild west sort of Wyatt Earp theme." She pulled in a deep breath. "What I'm trying to explain is we do not want to copy any of these shows. We want to find what will work here, for your state, your town, even your region. You don't want to put on a Las Vegas showgirls type thing if the people coming here are not looking for that type of entertainment."

Oscar leaned back from the table. "Tourists, budget, fits with our town." He tapped his fingers together in front of him. "This is going to open up a lot of jobs for our people. We want this place to be run well enough and be successful enough that we can pay these people a decent wage." He turned and looked at the men behind him and then at Fifer. "We will want this place to improve our economy but keep out the corruption that can go along with growth."

"A family-friendly place." Bill said, nodding his head. "I agree."

"I've driven around your town," Fifer said, ignoring the churning in her gut. Did they do any research at all on Louis McKenzie? Her father was a master at keeping his reputation above board, but there were signs of his true colors if you looked hard enough to find them. She turned from the computer screen to face the men. The Crestfield brothers had invited her father into this town. What would happen was on their heads, not hers.

48

"You have the restaurant as you come into the town and the hotel right off of the interstate. I've had a to-go plate of food from the hotel restaurant, and it was great." Fifer reached up and straightened the collar on her white silk blouse. "Other than that, are there any other shops or businesses that would draw people to this area? I need to learn why someone would want to stop in Red Creek on their way to and from the coast. Why here instead of the next town, or the town before this one?" She looked at their rather blank expressions. "Come on guys, give me something here."

"I have a great idea." Bill clapped his hands together and smiled down at Fifer. "You need to get to know this town, and Oscar needs to learn what it will take to make our little business work." He reached down and squeezed Oscar's shoulder. "Oscar, I want you to take Fifer to every store, shop, and business in Red Creek. Take her to eat at Olivia's and The Blue, take her to a high school basketball game, take her fishing on Red Creek, to the hunting lodge outside of town, to get a sausage dog at Eric's food truck. You can even take her to church one Sunday."

"I don't think that's exactly what she has in mind," Oscar said, frowning at the other men. "A trip to city hall with a map and a list of businesses will work a lot better."

"Or you can just tell me now while we are in here together talking." Fifer pulled her laptop closer to her. "I can take notes while you talk."

"No." Bill Crestfield rubbed his hands together. "You need to actually experience our little slice of heaven. You can't get to know us until you've lived among us. From now on, I expect to hear about where you went, how your information will work to improve the Red Creek image, and what we need to do to make this town more appealing to tourists. As a matter of fact." He looked at his watch. "Start now. Go to Olivia's for lunch. This place of ours is going to serve food. See what kind of food is putting us on the map."

"Do we have the budget for all this?" Oscar's eyes narrowed. "I don't eat out a lot, but I know you can run through some money."

"We have it covered," Bill said. "Use that credit card you have for expenses for something besides ink cartridges and pencils."

"Fifer, this is my sister, Olivia." Oscar pulled out the chair for Fifer to sit down in as his sister shook Fifer's hand. "She's in town working on the renovation the Crestfields are doing to the old movie theater. They want her to experience our town, whatever that means."

Olivia stepped over to where Oscar was pulling out his own chair and hugged her big brother. "Well, I'm glad you stopped by." She grinned down at Fifer, who had slid into the chair. "It's like pulling teeth to get him to come here to eat. He's sort of a tightwad."

Fifer smiled at the blond-haired woman with the silver-blue eyes. "You have a lovely place here. Oscar tells me this used to be some sort of factory?"

"It was the garment factory where a lot of the women around here used to work, our mother included. It shut down, and the building stood empty forever, sort of like the movie theater y'all are fixing up." Olivia looked around at the old brick walls with the exposed metal beams on the high ceilings.

"I think the place has a special charm, and knowing it's a part of the town's history makes it unique."

"See." Fifer looked over at Oscar. "Your sister understands what I'm trying to find for our place. We've got to find the right entertainment that will make the dinner theater stand out. We don't want another cookie cutter place you can find in any tourist town."

"Yeah, big brother." Olivia poked Oscar in the shoulder and winked. "Unique and classy, just like Red Creek."

"Don't you have something to do, like wash dishes or bus a table or something?" Oscar took the menu from the waiter, who stepped up beside Olivia. "We came here to get some of your outstanding southern cuisine that everyone is reading about."

"Aunt Sadie's glazed pork loin." Oscar looked at the menu. "That has to be good, or she wouldn't have her name on it."

"It is ah-maz-ing." Olivia leaned over Oscar's shoulder and looked at the menu. "Get it with the sweet potato soufflé and green pea salad."

"Yes, to the soufflé, no to the green peas." Oscar handed the menu to the waiter. "The pork loin, sweet potatoes, and fried okra." He looked at Fifer. "What about you?"

"I want the fried chicken, cheese potatoes with bacon, and I think I'll try the okra, too." She handed the menu to the waiter and looked at Oscar, who was staring with his eyebrows raised. "What?"

"I took you for a health nut," he said, picking up his water glass. "That's a nice sounding lunch."

"Don't let him aggravate you, Fifer." Olivia smiled. "You are going to love your lunch. And we have chocolate fudge cake on the menu for dessert, which I highly recommend. I've got to run, but I hope to see you around town."

"Thank you, Olivia." Fifer watched the other woman walk

away, then turned to Oscar. "What makes you think I'm a health nut?"

"Last night when you came to my backdoor, you looked like you'd been exercising."

"I had been. Is that unusual in Red Creek?"

"No." Oscar shrugged his shoulders and picked up the light gray napkin from the table and spread it on his lap. "Not at all. But you." He paused and stretched his eyes, taking in her face and upper body visible above the table. "You look like you take care of yourself. Not like somebody who eats a lot of fried chicken."

Fifer tilted her head slightly, mimicking Oscar's expression. "You, Oscar Robinson, don't look like someone who eats a lot of pork . . . but here we are." She picked up her napkin and spread it in her lap. "I like your sister. She doesn't favor you a lot. Is she your only sister?"

"She looks like our mother. I resemble our father, as you know. She's my only sister, but I have four brothers."

"And you are the oldest?"

"How did you guess?" Oscar took another sip of his water. The waiter came over with his tea and another glass of water for Fifer. "I'm the oldest, and Olivia is the youngest."

"It wasn't much of a guess. The oldest sibling is usually more serious, more . . . ." Fifer's eyes narrowed.

"Bossy?" Oscar grinned. "I believe that's the word you're looking for."

"Or opinionated." Fifer took a sip of her water.

"I take it you are the oldest too."

Fifer laughed, then coughed, taking another sip of water. "What are you insinuating?"

"I think you know." Oscar watched her blot the napkin to her lips. She could be nice if she wanted to, when she wasn't trying to show off her power. "Am I right?"

"Actually, I'm an only child, but you're right, I have strong opinions about certain things. Confidence and a steel backbone are required to work for Louis McKenzie."

"Even if you're the boss's daughter?"

"Especially if you're the boss's daughter."

Chapter Eight

Fifer leaned her head forward and squeezed her mane of red curls with the towel. Letting the tangled mess air dry would help keep down some of the frizz in this crazy Alabama humidity. Since arriving in Red Creek, it felt like her hair had expanded to three times its normal size, especially on rainy days like today. She flipped her head back, dropped the towel in the nearby hamper, and looked at her face in the bathroom mirror. What did Oscar Robinson see when he looked at her? He'd certainly seen a lot of her lately. Not here, in her home. Since she'd 'laid down the law,' as her father called it about Oscar's dog, the man nor the sweet four-legged neighbor had darkened her door. She'd watched them both from the shadows of her kitchen window when Oscar would take the animal out to do his business. The dog would race around their small yard, chase butterflies, bark for joy and roll in the grass like he had just escaped from Alcatraz and couldn't actually believe he was once again free.

Poor animal. Had she really relegated the creature to a prison sentence? She was fairly certain the dog had the run of Oscar's house. She could hear them through her walls, going up and down their stairs and moving around. How many times had she actually used the backyard to exercise? The idea had sounded good in her head, but man, her body was not wanting to work out in the heat and humidity. So far, the air-conditioned living room was as far as she'd made it with her mat.

Over the past week, since Bill Crestfield had insisted Oscar become her personal tour guide, they had gone out every afternoon to see different aspects of the little town, and the Red Creek natives seemed almost immune to the sauna like weather. The road leading from the interstate through the main part of town was getting a facelift, which was a good thing, but how did those men and women stand out in the sun and heat every day working on their equipment and flagging traffic without melting like the witch in the Wizard of Oz?

The smell of tar had filtered through the AC vents of Oscar's truck before the road work became visible. Oscar had decided after their lunch at his sister's restaurant that he would start his guided tour with a general ride around the county. They'd come up to orange cones blocking one side of the road, and a guy in an orange vest and a grey sweaty t-shirt stretched over his rotund middle holding a sign that said SLOW. He stood in the center of the pavement blocking their way. Instead of slowing down and letting the man wave his truck through the construction, Oscar had pulled over in the ditch behind one of the work trucks.

"What are you doing?" Fifer watched Oscar kill the engine. "You aren't planning on us walking back to the office, are you? There's bound to be a detour to get around this. Besides, didn't we come through this on our way to the restaurant?"

"Don't panic, your highness." Oscar unbuckled his seatbelt. "This won't take but a second. Come on."

Fifer unbuckled her seatbelt and stepped into the tall grass on the side of the road. The heel of her shoe slipped on a rock hidden in the overgrowth, and she grabbed the hot metal on the side of the truck to stop her stumble.

"You okay over there?" Oscar looked from where he was letting down his tailgate. "Watch out for snakes."

"Snakes?" Fifer looked down at her feet, then hurried around the truck bed. The man in the vest stepped out of the road and pulled off the yellow hard hat. Rivers of perspiration poured from his head and his short sandy colored hair was soppy wet.

"Red or orange?" Oscar lifted the lid of an enormous ice chest in the back of his truck and took out a couple of sports drinks. He handed one to the man, then took out several more. "Here." He pushed one in Fifer's direction.

"No, thank you." Fifer held up her hand like a stop sign and looked around at her feet again. "Are there really snakes around here?"

"Oh, yes' ma'am," the construction worker said, lowering the empty drink bottle from his lips. "We killed a rattler two days ago, every bit of four feet long." He tossed the plastic bottle in the back of Oscar's truck. "Thanks, man," he said to Oscar. "I'd better get back out there before somebody comes flying through here like they don't have good sense."

"See you, Doug." Oscar stuck the bottle in Fifer's direction again. "The drinks aren't for you. We're going to pass them out to these workers."

"Oh." Fifer took the ice-cold, wet bottle, then the next one, then the next one, and the next one from Oscar's hands. "I think this is all I can manage." She waited while Oscar filled his arms before following him onto the side of the road. "Why are we doing this?"

They walked down the side of the road to where several men with shovels in their hands were watching a dump truck pour asphalt onto a section they had already raked clean of the old potholed road. "Because it's hot and these people can't leave their jobs to go to the store."

Fifer smiled and passed out the drinks as Oscar spoke to each worker, calling every one of them by name and asking how they were doing or about a family member or something going on in their lives. They made two trips to his truck and back to the workers until everyone there had received something to drink.

"You're the lady that gave my brother all that nice house stuff." The man climbed down from the backhoe and took the drink from Fifer.

"No, Stevie." Oscar reached out and shook the sweaty man's hand. "This is Fifer McKenzie. She moved to town last week to work on the old movie theater project the Crestfields started up."

"I know, man." The road worker, Stevie, wiped his beefy forearm across his forehead. "Dalton helped move her in. He's working part time with that truck company and is usually put on the crew that is moving folks out of town, but the other day he helped unload this nice lady's stuff here in Red Creek." Stevie cracked the seal on the plastic bottle and unscrewed the lid. "She gave him a whole bunch of really nice things for the house. His wife and our momma were tickled pink. It was almost like Christmas."

"Really?" Oscar tilted his head to the side and raised an eyebrow.

"It was only a few things that didn't really fit my—personality." Fifer shifted her remaining drink from one hand to the other. "His brother was kind enough to take them when he finished unloading my boxes."

Oscar had gathered up the empty drink bottles from the workers on their way back through and tossed them in the back of his truck. They climbed in the cab and finally started to town. "I understand that it's hot, and they can't leave their jobs, but I'm sure they can bring water or their own drinks," Fifer said, turning the air conditioner vent on the dash toward her now damp face and neck. "Why did you stop and give them drinks from your cooler? You didn't have to, and I don't think anyone would think less of you if you just rode through the site like everyone else does."

"I guess for the same reason you gave Doug the house stuff." Oscar pulled a pair of aviator shades from his visor and slipped them on.

"I doubt that." Fifer looked over at her reflection in his sunglasses. Black mascara pooled under her eyes, making her look like a football player or an ancient warrior. She snatched open her purse and pulled out a tissue. "I didn't care what that man did with the things I gave him. I just didn't want them in my house."

"I went to college on a scholarship." Oscar eased the truck back onto the edge of the road and waited until the man with the SLOW sign waved him into the one lane of traffic. "It paid for the tuition and books, room and a meal ticket, but anything else I needed had to come out of my pocket. If I needed soap or deodorant or a candy bar, I had to work to get it."

"Your father couldn't help you; I suppose." Fifer flipped down the visor and looked in the little mirror. "Why didn't you tell me I looked like this?"

"Like what?" Oscar flashed her a smile, then turned his eyes back to the road. "No. Daddy had all the rest of the family to think about, and I would not ask for his help when I could make do on my own. I worked at car washes, lawn services, a construction company, any place where I could be outside and make a buck."

"Couldn't you get a job on campus?" Fifer blotted and wiped, smearing the eye makeup more as she mopped up what would come off her skin. "Ugh. I'm going to have to go home before I return to the office."

"That's fine. I need to let Festus out to go to the bathroom. I'll stop there, then go back to work." Oscar sped the truck up as they left the road construction area. "I was inside for classes and studying, for lifting weights for football. The only time I got to be outside was for practice and games. I hated that. I found jobs that would keep me outside. I remember a guy driving by one day when I was mowing a lady's lawn at straight up noon with a push mower. I was dying in the heat. This guy slowed his car, tossed a bottle of Gatorade to me out the window, and kept on going. That was one of the best drinks I ever had."

"So, you're sort of paying it forward?" Fifer looked over out of the corner of her eye. "Doing your good deed and all that?"

"Maybe." Oscar pulled the truck into his driveway. "I hadn't thought about it like that. I know what it's like to need a drink of water and have someone give you one when they don't have to. That's the type of person I want to be." He pulled his shades off and stuck them back in the visor. "Don't you?"

They got out of the truck and walked toward the front of the duplex. Festus barked on the other side of his door, and a pang of guilt stabbed at Fifer's insides. She'd never really thought about the kind of person she wanted to be. Not like that, anyway. How did Oscar see her? How did other people see her? More importantly . . . how did she see herself?

Fifer pushed the memory from earlier in the week down as her throat constricted. It was an overcast Sunday morning. Oscar and Festus had left Friday evening after work, and she hadn't seen them since then. He had said he would take her to church on Sunday morning if she wanted to go, but she'd declined his offer. The closest she'd been to church was at her meetings. She'd needed those meetings back then, like she needed her heart to beat, but as she'd grown stronger, gained control, learned how to cope with the cravings, she'd gone to the meetings less and less. She'd needed God then too, and He had been there for her. Now she was strong enough to make it without Him. She'd go to Oscar's church eventually, like the Crestfields wanted her to, but not yet. She pulled her mat out and headed downstairs. Right now, her father was nipping at her heels, making sure she was doing what he demanded. She had to keep her control, be strong, keep her distance. The last thing she needed right now was church.

She pushed the earbuds into place and stretched into her first pose. She would talk to Oscar about Festus. There was no need to make the dog stay inside if she wasn't going to use the backyard. She would just have to ignore the animal when it bumped on her backdoor. She could do that. No problem. She'd learned to ignore people a long time ago. Ignoring a dog would certainly be easier.

Chapter Nine

"When are you going to invite your girl to church and Sunday lunch?" Owen, one of Oscar's younger brothers and closest to him in age, sat in one of the rocking chairs on their father's front porch, careful not to spill his glass of tea.

"She's not my girl." Oscar sat down on the porch swing and gently nudged it with his cowboy boot. He had driven straight from his tent on the bank of Red Creek to his parents' house that morning to get ready for church. He returned there afterwards for their routine Sunday dinner. "I just work with the woman. I haven't seen her since I left the office Friday."

"Is that what the young folks are calling it nowadays? Work?" Lucy, Oscar's mother, sat down beside Oscar on the swing and winked at Owen. "I heard you've taken her out to eat and showed her around town."

"Not by choice." Oscar leaned forward and looked at Olivia, sitting on the front steps near her husband, Quinn. Their baby lay stretched out on Quinn's legs, content to watch her parents as she took her bottle. "I see you've been spreading my business around, sister."

"Don't look at me," Olivia said, throwing up her hands. "Although you have to admit that you being seen anywhere with a woman is big news. When was the last time you took a woman on a date? Not counting the one this week, of course."

"That was not a date." Oscar leaned back in the swing and clenched his jaw. Having a big family was good. Great actually, but if it was the Robinson family, you had to have thick skin. "I work with the woman, and the Crestfield brothers decided part of my job includes dragging her around Red Creek and letting her see what we have to offer tourists." He looked across the porch to Festus, trotting happily through the cow field toward the yard. He was sopping wet, with mud splattered to his fur and coating his legs. He must have decided to take a swim in the pond. "Believe me, Fifer doesn't like the situation any more than I do."

"Fifer?" Odi, Oscar's brother, who was number four in the Robinson pecking order and a lawyer, wrinkled his brow. "That's her name?"

"Not Fiver." Orville, Oscar's father, stepped through the screen door, guitar in his hand. "Fifer." He looked at Odi. "It's Scottish." He winked at his wife Lucy and walked over to the swing. "Get up, son, and let me sit by your momma." Oscar stood to let his father sit down. He stepped over to another rocking chair beside Owen. Orville settled into the swing. "I'm the one who told everybody about your little redhead. She seems like a spunky thing."

"She's not . . . oh never mind." Oscar rocked in his chair, listening to his father and mother sing some of the hymns everyone had already sung that morning in church. His parents loved hymns, but when out of the church house, always sang them with their own touch of country and blues.

Festus reached the yard and started up the front steps, but Olivia stopped him. "Oh, no you don't puppy." She put her hand on the muddy dog's nose, pushing him away from little

Maribel. "You stink like you've been rolling around in cow patties." She looked over her shoulder. "Oscar, control your dog."

Oscar stood and hopped off the edge of the porch. "Come on, boy. Let's go hose you off." He walked around the house, out of sight of the rest of the family, but still within hearing distance, the dog on his heels. His father and mother sang another song with some of his siblings joining in, then his mother must have taken the baby from Quinn. He listened as his father, who had been as stoic as a granite statue just a year ago until Oscar's mother returned to town, now laughed and talked baby talk to his granddaughter. What would it be like to find a woman who could affect him that much? A woman who could make him the happiest man around when she was near, but crush his very being for decades if she decided to go? If he found a woman like that, was getting to know her worth the risk? Orville Robinson sure seemed to think so—at least he did now that Lucy was back in his life—in their lives.

"Whoa, whoa, Festus!" Oscar stepped back as the dog shook from one end to the other, fiercely sending rivulets of brown water all over Oscar's jeans and white button-up shirt. It was like a shower from a muddy rain cloud. The dog trotted to the far edge of the yard and rolled around in the grass. Poor guy. Let him be a dog. He had to stay cooped up inside all day through the week because his neighbor might step foot in their backyard.

One thing was for sure. If a woman ever did come along who could turn his world upside down the way his mother had done to his father, she would be nothing like the redheaded drill sergeant living next door. Of that, he was certain.

‹───›

Fifer stepped out into the evening sun. The heat, ever present in the Alabama summer, was only a little more bearable this time of day. A soft breeze blew across the backyard and lifted a wisp of hair from her neck. Barking and Oscar's voice had drawn her outside. His truck had driven up a few minutes earlier as she was finishing her turkey sandwich. Where did he go every weekend? Did he have a second job?

"We're going to do this, boy, one way or the other."

Fifer's eyes crinkled with a smile. Oscar, on his knees over near the wooden fence that surrounded their yard, held a water hose in one hand with his other arm around his dog's neck and shoulders. The dog was in a metal tub, wiggling from one end to the other. Soap suds dripped from his gold fur as he licked his master's face, obviously ecstatic to have Oscar at eye level giving him hugs. Fifer walked across the yard, taking in Oscar's muscular, broad shoulders through the damp grey tee-shirt. Festus looked up and woofed, wiggling even more.

"I know I agreed to keep him out of the yard," Oscar said, looking over his shoulder, "but this is an emergency. He took a dip in the cow pond and is too filthy for the bathtub."

"That's okay." Fifer squatted down beside them. Festus pulled away from Oscar's stronghold and licked her face.

"Oh, no you don't." Oscar pulled the dog back, splashing soap suds and muddy water all over his chest. "Our neighbor has no desire to smell like a cow barn." He dropped the water hose into the metal tub and fished out a big yellow sponge. "You probably need to go back inside if you don't want him to bother you. He doesn't mean anything by it, but he's a dog, and he's going to be friendly."

"About that." Fifer pressed her lips together, catching the insinuation that as a human she was not very friendly. "I was being selfish and perhaps a little rude to ask you to keep John . . . I mean Festus out of the yard. It is your yard too, after all."

Oscar fished the water hose from the tub and began rinsing the soap off Festus, not saying anything or looking in her direction. "So." Fifer tilted her head to the side, where she could better see his face in the dimming sun. "I want you to let Festus come and go as he pleases out here, like he did when I first moved in. Okay?"

Oscar finished rinsing the dog, holding on to his collar as the animal leaned away, straining to get to Fifer. "Are you one hundred percent sure? He's not going to change his behavior any time soon. I've potty trained him, and he's doing better with not jumping up on people, but he's going to love on you if you're around. I can't stop that."

"Yes." Fifer grinned. The dog was lovable, like an overgrown toddler. "He and I will be fine." She reached out and touched the happy animal's nose.

"Festus, no!" Festus jerked away from Oscar's grip, encouraged by Fifer's hand. He bounded over the edge of the metal tub, turning it over, and sending the soapy water into the grass. The dog flew onto Fifer's chest, sending her flying backwards, sandwiching her between the soapy, wet ground and his soppy, wet body. Festus flopped on top of Fifer, spread eagle, licking her face and neck with abandon. Oscar jumped up, kicking the tub out of the way. He leaned over and grabbed the slippery, wet dog around the middle. "Get off the woman, Festus!"

Oscar pulled back, his feet slipping in the suds and puddles. His feet shot up as he flew backwards on his rear,

Festus landing on top of him. The dog squirmed free and flipped over to face his owner. He licked him once for good measure, then bounded away toward the other side of the yard. "I'm really sorry." Oscar sat up and looked in Fifer's direction. She continued to lie flat on her back, her shoulders shaking. "Hey." Oscar crawled over the soppy grass to her side. "Don't cry. He didn't hurt you, did he?"

Fifer opened her eyes. Oscar's face frowned down at her, his eyes narrow with concern. Water dripped from his nose and splattered onto her forehead. The laughter she'd been trying to hold in rose higher in her chest, and she cackled out loud, then snorted. "You look like a drowned rat."

A grin slowly spread across Oscar's face. "And you, Fifer McKenzie, just snorted like a hog." He stood and reached his hand down. "Are you okay? I thought he had hurt you when you just laid there and didn't move."

"I'm fine." Fifer took his wet, slippery hand, and a slight tingle ran up her arm. She swallowed and looked away from his intense gaze and clingy wet shirt. "He knocked the breath out of me, but all the licking and water and soap, and watching your face when he got away . . . you have to admit all of this was funny."

"I can see the humor in it." Oscar pulled her up but didn't let go of her hand. "I just wasn't so sure you could."

Heat ran up from under Fifer's black tank top to her neck and inched toward her face. She pulled her hand away and looked at Festus, lifting his leg on the fence on the opposite side of the yard near her matching water hose. "I know I seem . . . solemn at times, but I have my reasons." Her voice dropped to little more than a whisper. "I'm really a nice person once you get to know me. At least . . . I think I am." She looked back at Oscar and pulled in a deep breath. His eyes darted away, and she glanced down at her tank top, looking like a second skin stretched tight over her torso. "I guess I better get inside and change." She pinched the wet fabric at her mid-section, pulling the clinging tank top away from her body with some difficulty. She released her hold and an air bubble held the material out. She looked up. Oscar's eyes burned into her, watching her every move in the twilight. "I'll see you tomorrow." She turned and walked toward her back patio.

"Fifer." Oscar's voice cut through the quickly falling darkness. Fifer turned and looked where he continued to stand. "You have a nice laugh. You should use it more often."

Chapter Ten

O scar rolled over in bed and punched his pillow. Would this night ever end? Festus snored softly from his bed in the corner. One of the hardest lessons the dog ever learned was to sleep in his own bed. Oscar loved his dog, but he was a large man. Festus wasn't fully grown, and he was already a big boy. There wasn't room for both of them in his queen-sized bed, and a king would not fit in this bedroom. Besides, the second time he woke up with dog behind in his face, he decided it was time for a change.

He couldn't blame the lack of sleep tonight on Festus. No, his lack of sleep tonight was solely because of the redhead with the astonishingly well developed set of curves living next door. He'd noticed she was nice looking before. He wasn't a monk. Despite all the ragging and picking his siblings liked to throw his way, he had relationships with females. Not in a while, and not anything serious, but he had female friends. If he was honest, he'd noticed how nice these women looked too. What red-blooded male wouldn't? Fifer McKenzie, however, was getting under his skin, and he did not like it—not at all.

It had been a long week. First, finding out he was supposed to cater to her whims. *Remember to look into that.* Being forced to traipse around town with the woman for everyone to see was a bit irritating. Folks would see them together and assume things. His family was obviously doing just that. Worse than all that, though, was this evening. Until now, she had been sort of prickly and stuck up. Granted, his brothers, especially Owen and Ori, accused him numerous times over the years of being a snob. He wasn't. He just didn't have time for stupidity. That wasn't snobbery. The difference was obvious, and Fifer McKenzie was a snob.

This evening, when she let out that unladylike snort, and then later when she sounded all . . . what? Vulnerable? *I'm really a nice person once you get to know me. At least . . . I think I am.* She'd sounded almost like she wasn't sure whether she considered herself nice at all. That Fifer McKenzie was a completely different woman from the bossy one who put him in his place several times throughout the week, standing up to him and anyone else who confronted her. He would like nothing more than to punt bossy Fifer McKenzie into the next county.

The woman he'd seen tonight, the human version . . . she was keeping him awake. Standing in the backyard in soaking wet in clothes that fit like a second skin, blushing like a schoolgirl, that girl, no woman—definitely woman—she would not get out of his head.

Which one was the real one? It didn't matter, at least not to him. She would be gone when she finished the project. That was a good thing. He had a plan for his future. He was not going to be in the Crestfield office crunching numbers and running projects for the rest of his life. That thought alone was enough to make him break out in a cold sweat. No, Fifer would move on, the dinner theater would be a success, and he would continue to put back his money to make his own dream come true.

A sound out the window in his back yard drew Oscar's attention. He got up, glancing over at Festus, who continued to snore, and stepped to the window. He looked down from the second story to the shadowy figure moving slowly in the moonlight. She really was beautiful, no denying that. He stared, unable to draw his eyes away as she worked through one stretch and exercise pose to another, each graceful, almost like a dance. She wasn't sleeping either. He continued to watch her, even when she was done, and sat motionless in the grass. Who was this woman? Why did she feel the need to be so domineering to everyone? What part of her life made her that way?

After a few minutes of sitting in the grass, legs crossed with her face turned upward, almost like she was praying, she stood and looked up at his window. He pulled back into the shadows. Had she seen him? No, it was dark. *You shouldn't have been spying on her.* He ignored the voice in his head. She eventually turned away and walked back into her side of the duplex. Oscar walked over and sat on the bed. He picked up his phone and looked at the time. Four-thirty, close enough to six. There was no way he was going back to sleep now.

He flipped on his bedside lamp and picked up his Bible to do his morning reading. Casting all your anxieties on Him, because he cares for you. Oscar bowed his head. It would be a long day, probably a long week, possibly a long six months, but God was in control. Whatever happened, God was in control. *Lord, this isn't my plan, but I know you have a purpose in mind, so I'm giving today and every day to You.*

What do you take in your coffee?

Fifer chewed on her bottom lip and stared at her phone. She backed out the text message to Oscar and laid the phone on her bed. She looked at her cell phone one more time. Seven o'clock. She would leave soon. There wasn't a coffee shop in Red Creek, or if there was, she hadn't stumbled upon it yet. There was, however, halfway decent coffee at the gas station on the way to the office with a surprising array of flavored creamers and syrups.

She'd been up since, well, pretty much all night. When she came in yesterday evening after being bowled over by Festus, she'd taken a long hot bath, which was not her style. Normally, she was a shower person. Hop in, hop out, get on with your life, but getting the full body hug from the drenched dog had left her pretty grungy. That wasn't the true reason for lounging in the tub. No. The hot soak had been an attempt to deal with what had happened to her insides.

The way Oscar smiled at her, the way he'd looked at her, and worse yet, the way she'd reacted. That's what started the night long battle for control. That, and the questions that seemed to keep finding their way into her head. She'd filled the tub with steamy water, grabbed the luffa, and scrubbed herself down. The stimulation of the hot water and scrubbing every inch of her skin had made her feel alive, but not nearly alive as she had been in the backyard. That feeling. That was something she'd forgotten existed. Forgotten because it wasn't allowed, not for Louis McKenzie's daughter anyway.

After the soak, she'd climbed in the bed. It had only been eight o'clock, but her body and mind thought it was much later. The emotional high of the backyard had been wonderful. The pitiful low that followed during the bathtub, the self-examination, the why and why not that followed every fresh memory of the evening had drained her dry. She'd climbed out of the bathtub and slept until midnight, if you could call it sleep. The dreams, flashes really, had been almost as bad as anything she'd experienced all those years ago in rehab.

In the most vivid dream, a crowd of people were gathered on the side of the road, like the road the maintenance crew was working on earlier in the week. Her father was there, people she'd worked with over the years, people she'd known as a child, people from Red Creek, and, of course, Oscar. Her grandmother and even her mother were standing in the crowd, and they were all looking at something on the ground.

Fifer had walked up, dressed in her best work suit, her hair actually staying in place for once, and pushed her way through the crowd of people. Looking down, there she was, another Fifer, the real Fifer, laying on the side of the road covered in mud and filth. It was like Festus had been when she first walked to her backyard and saw Oscar bathing the animal, only her mud and dirt were dried and caked on much, much deeper. The pool of slime sucking her to the earth. That wasn't the worst part. A snake, an enormous python like she'd seen in the zoo as a child, slithered languidly across her neck and was wrapping around her body.

She'd looked around at the people all watching her. Some, like her father, had laughed at her as she tried to move out of the stench and away from the snake. Others, like Oscar and her grandmother, watched with pity, or maybe it was compassion, but still, they just watched. She'd wanted to scream at the people, at the snake, but no words would come. She squatted down and reached forward. If no one else would help her, then she'd help herself. She'd reached for the slimy Fifer's arm, but it slipped from her grasp. Filthy Fifer started sinking into slimy mud, the weight of the snake pulling her down. Fight it, her mind screamed to her other self, but the other Fifer either didn't want to fight, or she couldn't. The watching Fifer looked around in panic. There had to be someone who could help.

Fifer had awakened from the dream in a cold sweat, drenched from head to toe. She needed help, wanted to fall into her old habits worse than she had wanted anything since her father drug her into the rehab hospital almost a decade before. She would have found the help she craved if it hadn't been the middle of the night, and everything in this mom and pop town shut down at sunset.

Thank goodness she kept to her diehard rule—no temptations in the home, not even cough syrup or mouth wash. If Listerine had been in her medicine cabinet, she would have downed the entire bottle, then went looking for more. Instead, she'd gone downstairs and eaten three cups of chocolate pudding, all the pudding in the cabinet.

Back in the day, she would have called Rob, her sponsor for the first five years after she'd gotten clean. After another five years of sobriety though, she'd began calling him less and less. She'd finally gotten a handle on her life, gained control of her own sleeping monster. She'd built a wall, shoved down any and all emotion that would trigger a slip toward her own personal pit, and not let anything or anyone put a crack in her armor.

Until yesterday evening in the backyard with a goofy dog and a laughing neighbor. They were good, not bad. Weren't bad feelings supposed to drive her down? How come a good thing, a good feeling, a good person, had brought on the nightmares . . . the needs? This debate had raged in her head on the living room floor, swirling round and round while the ear buds filled her mind with her lovely, calming music. She tried stretching and cardio; her tried-and-true way to get her head back on straight, but this time, they failed.

Like a caged animal needing freedom, she'd finally went outside. The stars above, the breeze, the almost full moon shining down had been a kiss on her soul. Crickets chirped as she stretched out flat on her back in the grass, damp with dew. "God, are You there?" The words slipped from her lips in a whisper as she stared into the night. "Is it true what they said at the meetings? If it's true and You are there . . ." She paused, swallowing hard. "Help me. I don't want to be that woman in the dream. Either one of them."

The night continued, the breeze barely blew, the crickets serenaded, nothing changed. Slowly, Fifer sat up and started going through her poses again, letting the night and its calmness flow over her. Had God answered her prayers, or had she finally overcome the monster one more time? It didn't matter.

When she came in an hour later, she'd showered before laying on the bed. Am I a nice person? The question moved to the front of her brain, forcing her to answer. No, not if that saying 'pretty is as pretty does' had an ounce of truth to it. She was ugly to the bone if her actions and her words meant anything at all. Could she be a nice person? Who knew? A sliver of dread ran down her spine. *Can I be a nice person and not fall into my pit, not be swallowed up by my cravings?*

Some time later, she rolled over and stared at the window, the morning sun's rays bringing in another day. *Is what I've become just a monster of a different kind?* The thoughts rolled around in her head as she got dressed and put on her make-up. At seven-thirty, she grabbed her phone where she had dropped it before. There was a better way. She could be a decent person, not as nice as Oscar, but at least decent. She could keep everything inside controlled and still be friendly on the outside . . . somehow.

> What do you take in your coffee?

She hit send before her fears took over. "I can be a good person. I have good in me. Somewhere."

Chapter Eleven

O scar accepted the coffee from Fifer's outstretched hand and took a sip. "Thank you." He stifled a yawn, rising in his throat. "I'll need this to help me stay focused." He raised his eyelids over the paper cup and watched Fifer. Her eyes remained fixed on the papers he'd spread out on the conference table. She must not have seen him watching her through his window, or either didn't want to talk about them both being up all hours of the night. "Take a seat." He set down the coffee cup and motioned to the chair next to his. "We need to go over these estimates. The exterminator finished checking the place for rodents and did another termite check." He slid a paper in her direction as he sat down. "My dad is supposed to start cleaning the junk out today."

"Your father?" Fifer's brow creased, and she turned to Oscar. "I understand you wanting to help your father out, but I feel we need to hire a professional to do the clean-up." She rubbed her lips together, and her mouth turned up in an uneasy smile. "What I mean is, it looks like it will be a big job, more than one man can handle in the timeframe we need."

Well, that was different. The coffee and the explanation

about a decision instead of the usual barking orders and expecting to be obeyed. What was she up to? "Actually, my father is a professional."

"He may be a janitor or custodian." Fifer paused and lifted her hands. "And there's nothing wrong with those things at all, but that doesn't mean he is equipped to do this job." She raised her fingers to her face and tapped her lips. "We can talk to whoever we hire to clean out the place and get your father on the work crew, if you think that will help him out."

Oscar watched Fifer's fingertips touch her lips, and something in his middle tightened. He blinked and pulled his eyes away from her mouth. He picked up his coffee. What had she said? He smiled. "My father isn't a janitor. He's a junkman. I promise you, he can handle the job."

"A junkman? Like Fred Sanford from the seventies?"

"Pretty much." Oscar's smile stretched wide. It was kind of fun shocking her, watching her squirm in this new polite role she was playing. "I've already talked to Bill and Grant. They signed off on it, but of course I have to run everything by you for approval first."

"I think I want to talk to your father before I sign off, as you say." Fifer moved her hips in the chair. "He will need to give us an estimate and sign the standard work agreement, making sure he gets everything done and, to my—our satisfaction." She looked down at the papers on the table, her fingers shifting them around as she spoke. "If he doesn't live up to his end of the agreement, we will have to let him go. Are you sure you want to involve your family in business? It can sometimes be . . ." she looked up at Oscar. "Unpleasant. I would hate to see you hurt your father's feelings."

Oscar squeezed his lips together so the drink of coffee in his mouth wouldn't spew across the table. He swallowed and looked at Fifer, merriment filling his eyes. "Believe me, the last thing you need to worry about is hurting Orville Robinson's feelings." He chuckled and set down the empty coffee cup. "That sappy man you saw the other day at the movie theater has a mind like a steel trap and a spine as stiff as, well, as stiff as yours."

"Well." Fifer's eyes narrowed and her tone changed to the drill sergeant Oscar was more familiar with. "I want to talk with him. Draw up the work agreement and set up a meeting at the site. If he can do the job, fine. If he can't, you can tell him, and we will look somewhere else."

"Hey." Oscar tilted his head, trying to catch the woman's eye. "I'm sorry. I'm not laughing at you." He watched her jaw clench. "Really, I'm not. It's just you do not know my father. The idea of hurting Orville Robinson's feelings over a business decision is sort of preposterous."

"That's fine." Fifer turned and looked at him from the corner of her eye, her chin tilting upward. "But I still want to talk to him."

Great, Oscar. You wanted the dragon queen back, well here she is. "That's no problem. I'll give him a call. We can probably meet with him this morning."

"Good." Fifer pushed her chair back from the table and stood. "I'll be back in a few minutes. Get the meeting set up before I return."

Oscar watched her march from the room. Had he hurt her feelings? Naah, that wasn't possible. Should he apologize again when she came back, or would that make her madder? He pulled his cell from his pocket. He'd better let it go. He rolled his eyes as he punched in his father's number. Of all the people in Red Creek to worry about hurting their feelings, she picked Orville Robinson. "Hey, Dad. Fifer wants to talk to you about the junk in the theater before you start the job."

"Sure, son. I want to talk to her again anyway. Why don't you bring her by the store?"

"Maybe another time. Can you meet us at the theater in about thirty minutes?"

"I can do that."

"Great." Oscar paused. "She can be a little demanding when it comes to work, Dad."

"She wants the job done right, Oscar. There's no shame in that. That's part of what makes her a good businesswoman. I'll see you in thirty minutes."

Oscar said goodbye and hung up the phone. No, if anybody could hold their own with Fifer McKenzie, it would be his father. Oscar straightened the papers on the table, the coffee starting to kick in. As a matter of fact, this morning might turn out to be entertaining. Let the real Fifer McKenzie meet the real Orville Robinson. This was going to be fun.

Fifer gently ran her fingers under her eyes and took a deep breath. She turned the handle and stepped back into the conference room. Oscar looked up from his chair. "Is everything set up?" she asked, walking over to the table.

"He will meet us there in thirty minutes." Oscar said, staring at her face. "Does that work for you?"

"Yes." Fifer reached up and rubbed the corner of her eyes. Could he tell she had cried? "I'm going to have to start taking an allergy pill. Something in Red Creek is making my eyes water." *Not something, someone.* She pulled her chair out and sat down. "Let me read over the rest of these papers, and I will be ready to go. It shouldn't take but a few minutes."

"Fifer, I really am sorry for laughing." Oscar's voice was

soft. "I wasn't laughing at you. I was laughing at the idea of my father being soft enough to need protecting."

"It's fine." Fifer picked up one of the papers and pretended to look it over. "I'm just a little touchy today."

"My sister got that way too." Oscar said, leaning back in his chair. "She would bite all our heads off. But the good part was, she would cook all kinds of desserts then too."

Fifer's lips pushed into a firm line. She set the paper down and looked at Oscar. "What?"

"My sister Olivia. You met her at her restaurant."

"I know *who* you are talking about." Fifer's words came out slowly, like she was speaking to someone who didn't understand English. "I just don't know *what* you are talking about?"

"She would get all touchy-feely every month, too." He shrugged. "Like you are today, and yesterday."

"What do you mean, touchy feely?" Fifer's eyes glared at Oscar. "I am not on my period, if that's what you're implying."

"Oh." Oscar's lips puckered like he was ready to whistle the Star-Spangled Banner. "My mistake." He shrugged his shoulders. "But you have to admit that yesterday and now today, too, you've been acting sort of weird."

"Weird?" Fifer's eyes stretched. "You think I'm acting weird?"

"Not weird in general. Just weird for you."

"For your information." Heat flared in Fifer's cheeks, and her voice grew harder. "I was trying to be nice to you. That obviously backfired if you thought I was acting weird and was on my period. And let's get things straight right here and now." She leaned forward and poked her finger toward his chest. "Women can have a period without getting all touchy-feely, as you call it, or baking brownies. Your sister was probably a young teen when she was doing this, not a grown woman. Teens are still children. Girls and boys alike get all touchy-feely in their teens. I imagine you weren't always a bouquet of roses at that age either."

"Okay, okay." Oscar held his hands up in surrender. "Geesh. I'm sorry. You are not having a period, and I was wrong."

"Actually." Fifer pulled away from his chair and tugged on her blouse. "I lied. I am having my period. That's not why I'm acting weird. I didn't sleep last night. I had a horrible dream. I'm sure that never happens to you, but it does to me. That's why I'm a hot mess and why I may be a tiny bit emotional." She pulled in a deep breath. "Now. Let's start over."

"And forget this conversation ever happened," Oscar said, pulling his chair closer to the table.

"Yes. Exactly." Fifer picked up the papers again and tried to focus on the work in front of her. After a couple of minutes of complete silence, she set them down again. "Can I ask you something?"

"Yes," Oscar said slowly, like a snake charmer talking to a cobra.

"How do you know how to be like this?"

"Like what?"

"Like, nice. I tried to be nice to you, and you laughed at me and acted like I was weird. I don't think you are weird when you are nice. You seem to be nice all the time, like it comes naturally to you."

"Ha." Oscar laughed again, and Fifer's eyes narrowed. "I'm not laughing at you," he said, holding his hands up again. "I'm laughing at the idea of me being nice all the time. My family, especially my siblings, would strongly disagree with that assumption. Believe me."

"You seem nice enough to me. Except, of course, when we first met, and you were an obnoxious pig."

"Yeah." Oscar grinned. "Except for that."

"You were." Fifer's lips pulled up at the corners. "See, I insulted you, and you're still nice. I would have had to put you in your place again if you had said something like that to me."

"True." Oscar rubbed his hand along his jaw. "I've never given any of this a lot of thought, but I guess I would ask you why are you not nice?"

"Because." Fifer stopped, and her eyes searched the room. "I think." She drug out the words, her gaze returning to Oscar. "I guess I've associated sternness and meanness with power, and niceness with weakness." Queasiness washed through her gut. "I'm an obnoxious bully, aren't I?"

"You're not always obnoxious," Oscar joked. He looked at her sad eyes, and his tone changed. "You're all business, that's all."

"But I'm all business, even when I'm not discussing business."

"You don't have to be." Oscar reached out to touch her shoulder, but pulled his hand back. "You can change. You were trying to change a while ago, and I made fun of you for it. That is on me, not you, and I'm sorry."

Fifer pulled in a deep breath. "Change is hard."

"Yes. But most things worth doing are hard and scary too. If you really want to change, I'm going to start praying for it to happen."

"I'm sorry." Fifer wiped her eyes. "You're my work associate, not my high school guidance counselor or my spiritual advisor." She pushed her chair back. "We'd better get going. I don't want to be late for a meeting I insisted on having."

"Fifer." Oscar reached out his hand to her arm. "There's no reason why we can't be friends. This." He lifted his hand and moved his finger between the two of them. "Is what friends do. Talk about things that matter to them, say what they think, apologize when they are wrong, and yes, pray for each other."

Fifer looked toward the door, away from Oscar's blue eyes breaking down her strategically built walls. "I'm not sure I'm friend material," she said, scared to look his way.

"I'm willing to take the risk, if you are."

Fifer listened to the chair pushing back as Oscar stood. She turned and looked up at him. "Let me think about it. This seems easy to you, but you don't know me."

"But God knows you, are like I said." Oscar smiled softly. "I'm willing to try this if you are.

Chapter Twelve

"We have lights now." Oscar flipped the switch inside the theater lobby. "And boy, do we have junk."

"It's a good thing junk is my specialty," Orville Robinson said, rubbing his hands together, a broad smile stretching across his face. "Son, you see junk. I see opportunity."

"I see a lot of hard work." Fifer stepped to the side to let Oscar's father move deeper into the cluttered room.

"Work is a good thing, Miss Fifer." Orville picked up a stack of plastic tumblers crammed inside a cardboard box. He rubbed off a layer of the grime clinging to everything in the room with his thumb and looked at a tumbler. "I remember when they were using these." He held up the glass and pointed to the Raiders of the Lost Ark emblem on the side. "I bet a lot of other people will, too."

Oscar stepped over to where Fifer was studying his father. "I wasn't joking when I said he was a junkman. He'll get a crew to load all this stuff up and take it to the salvage yard behind his shop. Then he'll go through it all and see what he can turn a profit on, what needs to be donated somewhere, and what goes in the dumpster or the recycle bin."

Fifer's eyes followed Orville methodically moving from pile to pile. He would pick up one thing and grunt, then drop it, pick up another and smile like he'd discovered a diamond. "He must have a large operation if he actually made enough money to raise a family doing this sort of thing."

"It's the largest in Red Creek." Oscar continued to keep his eyes on his father, careful not to glance over at Fifer, his face wearing a business as usual look.

"Let me guess." Fifer turned to Oscar, her eyes narrow. "It's the only junk business in Red Creek."

"Yes, that would be right." Oscar grinned and looked at Fifer. "Don't you call that marketing strategy? State the fact, but put a grand and exciting spin on it?"

"You can call it that if you want to." She smiled as Orville's head bobbed down behind the counter at the back of the room. "He sure seems to be enjoying himself."

"He's been a junk man his entire life, and yeah, he seems to really enjoy it. I think it's sort of a nostalgia thing for him. Plus, he says every new venture is like a real-life treasure hunt. When we were kids, he came across a box of costumes at an estate sale. For about two years, every time he took us with him to pick up anything, me and my brothers all wore these dinky felt pirate hats."

"It sounds like you had a nice childhood." Fifer adjusted her purse on her shoulder. "I'm impressed. He found what he enjoyed doing and made a living out of it. I would guess the junk business wouldn't be such a lucrative venture, especially in such a small town."

"It's not. Owen and Ori finally brought him into the modern age with an online store last year. Before that, and even since then, the store has barely stayed afloat."

"You grew up . . ." Fifer paused.

Oscar looked from where his father popped back up from behind the counter with a box. A famous movie logo mouse smiled from the side of the container. Oscar turned to Fifer. "I grew up poor." He twisted his lips to the side. "At least we thought we were poor." He shook his head. "No. That's not right. We had enough food and clothes and everything. As kids, we never knew any difference and didn't give it much consideration, but I saw how much Dad struggled, especially when I got into my teens."

"I'm sure there were hard times, but it still sounds nice." Fifer's brow furrowed as Orville open the doors to the theater room. "Should we follow him?"

"Naah," Oscar said as his father disappear through the velvet covered double doors. "Unless you just want to. He'll remember we are here and be back in a minute or two." He stepped over to a couple of five-gallon buckets, dumped out the rags and papers onto the dusty floor and flipped them over. "Have a seat. I know your feet have got to be hurting in those shoes." He followed Fifer's eyes down to her heels. She was a tall woman, five-ten, but she wore two or three-inch heels to work. Did she wear those sorts of shoes to look her coworkers in the eye or possibly stare down at them? It was probably effective when she was making a point about something. She definitely liked to make a point.

"I've been wearing these types of shoes so long that I barely notice the strain they put on my feet." Fifer stepped over to the buckets and carefully sat down beside Oscar. "How did your mother feel about your father being a junk man? Did she go on your little adventures, too?"

Oscar's lips turned down. "No." He looked past Fifer to the front door, now behind them. The smell of the closed-up room filled the place, damp and dusty, sort of like all his childhood memories. There were a lot of good times, like he had shared, but there was definitely heartache, too. He didn't talk about the hard times. They were over and in the past. He looked back at Fifer. The sunlight filtered through the dirty glass doors, cascading through the dust. "She wasn't around back then."

"Oh." Fifer looked around and pulled in a deep breath. "My mother died when I was a teenager."

"I'm sorry." Oscar watched Fifer glance down at her hands, not meeting his gaze. He looked at the red curls stretched tight across her head to the bun she wore at the base of her neck, pulled tight and pinned down in perfect control, just like the rest of her.

"Thank you," she whispered. She raised her eyes and looked ahead. "I don't like to talk about it."

"I get it. You don't have to." Oscar gently placed a hand on her shoulder. She tensed for only a second, then relaxed, not pulling away. His eyes followed the silhouette of her face along her cheek, down to where her lips parted, her teeth pulling in the bottom one. She did that when she was thinking—not paying attention to the people around her.

"I can get this done by the date you want," Orville said, strolling back through the velvet doors, clapping his hands together. "Oh." He stopped and looked from Oscar to Fifer. "Excuse me. Seems I interrupted a meeting." He grinned a Cheshire cat grin. "Or something."

"No." Oscar dropped his hand and bounced up. Fifer rose beside him, but slower, not like she had a spring under her seat the way he had. "We were talking about the junk business while we waited for you to check out everything. I told Fifer I was sure you could get it all done." *I'm rambling.* Oscar clamped his lips together.

"Oscar tells me you have a store and a salvage yard." Fifer pushed her skirt down into its proper place. She glanced at the hem a good bit above her knees, then up at Orville. "Would you mind if I see it?"

Oscar turned and looked at Fifer, his forehead wrinkled. She didn't have that know-it-all appearance he'd seen a few times when he'd tried to explain a spread sheet to her, and she wasn't smirking. She seemed genuinely interested in his father's business. "It's nothing special, really. Not anything like you see on those cable shows or 'Antiques Roadshow.'"

"Don't listen to him." Orville walked over to where they waited, fishing a piece of butterscotch candy from his pocket. "As far as junk stores go, I think mine is topnotch."

"I'm sure it is, and I would enjoy seeing it." Fifer smiled. "If you are okay with what we've decided, I will print off the work agreement and we . . . ." She stopped and looked at Oscar, his head tilted to the side, eyebrows squished together, staring at her like she had grown a third eye. "Or I—can come by after lunch and have you sign it."

"No," Oscar said slowly. "I want to come too."

"Good." Orville slapped his son on the back, then looked at Fifer. "Before you draw up those papers, I need to talk to you. There are a few things I've already found in here that may be worth a nice little chunk of change."

"Really?" Fifer looked around at the piles of junk. "Are you sure?"

"Oh yes. I'm sure." Orville unwrapped the candy and popped it into his mouth. "I'll set those items to the side. The way I usually handle these things is I sell the profitable pieces on consignment, then take a small percentage of what the owner makes on the item. Now, if you want to handle it differently, that is fine too. I can buy the items outright, and you won't have to risk them not selling."

"No." Fifer's eyes connected with Orville's and held. "You realize that you could have sold everything in here and kept all the money. We would have never been the wiser. It would have been perfectly legal, according to the work agreement."

"Just because something's legal doesn't always make it right, now does it, Miss Fifer?"

"No, Mr. Robinson." Her mouth flattened into a straight line. "It certainly doesn't. I appreciate your honesty. Thank you." Her expression cleared, and she smiled. "Call me Fifer, please, without the Miss."

"You're welcome, Fifer. But to be honest, I didn't do it because of you." Orville shoved the empty candy wrapper into the worn pocket of his jeans. "I enjoy getting a good night's sleep," he said, winking at her. "Some people say I can be a bear if I don't get my rest." He jerked his head toward Oscar. "If I lied and cheated you or anybody else out of money that was rightfully theirs, I'd be pacing the floor all night long until I made things right. Sinning doesn't set well with my soul."

Orville said goodbye after that with the promise to meet them after lunch at Robinson Junk and Salvage. The encounter had gone completely different from what Oscar expected. Oscar's mother said Orville Robinson was a charmer back in the day and could be again if he wanted. Apparently, the man never wanted to before—until now. "Are we done here?" he asked, looking back at Fifer.

"Yes, I believe so." Fifer picked up her designer leather bag she had set on one of the buckets. "I really like your father. That part about cheating and lying not setting well with his soul, it's interesting. He's interesting."

"If you like interesting, you need to meet the entire Robinson clan." Oscar held the front door of the theater open, and Fifer walked through. "And just so you know, Dad was on his best behavior for you."

"He seemed sincere." Fifer waited while Oscar locked the door. "Do you think he was lying to me?"

"Definitely not." Oscar turned and dropped the theater keys into Fifer's hands. "He's as honest as the day is long. All I mean is." Oscar rubbed his hand along his jawline. "He is not usually so nice."

"He's a bully like me?" Fifer put the keys in her purse, and they started toward her Miata. Oscar had wanted to come in his truck, but she'd insisted they use her car. "I wouldn't have thought that."

"No." Oscar opened the passenger's door and crammed his large frame into the petite car. Thank goodness Ori was in Nashville. If the family clown ever saw him riding around in this girly car, he would never hear the end of it. His other brothers would hassle him enough if they found out, but nobody could aggravate him like Ori. "Dad is just extremely plainspoken. He usually says what needs to be said and doesn't care what people think. At least that's the way he was before he got married last fall."

"Is that what I am?" Fifer looked over at Oscar as she started the little sports car. "Plain spoken?"

"No. You're more—and don't take this the wrong way—calculated." He watched Fifer's face, but she didn't seem to be mad at his words. "I think you put thought into the way you act. You come across as bossy because you are trying to. Dad is just a natural, I don't know, grouch?"

"He certainly wasn't grouchy a few minutes ago." Fifer pulled a pair of oversized sunglasses from her purse and slipped them onto her face. "He reminded me of you."

"Everybody says I resemble him the most out of all the kids."

Fifer stopped backing out of the parking lot and looked over at Oscar. "Yes, you definitely look like your father, but that's not what I meant. You are a good person, and he is, too. In my life, good people aren't as plentiful as they seem to be in yours."

Oscar looked at Fifer, her expression hidden behind the

shades. "That's a shame." His phone buzzed, and he slipped it from his pocket. "Excuse me a second."

Fifer turned back to the steering wheel and started to the office. Oscar slid the green button on his phone. "Hey, Odi. What's up?"

"Dad said your friend, the redhead, her last name is McKenzie."

"Yeah," Oscar said slowly, turning his face away from Fifer.

"I bumped into Bill Crestfield a while ago, and he said she's Louis McKenzie's daughter. The bigwig real estate guy in Birmingham."

"That's his name." Oscar glanced over at Fifer, but she wasn't paying any attention to his phone call. "Why?"

"Be careful, Oscar. This guy puts on a good front, but he has a shady side. I'm surprised the Crestfields went into business with him."

"Are you sure?"

"I'm sure. I've got to run, but you may want to poke around in what the Crestfields are getting into."

"Thanks, brother." Oscar slipped his phone back in his pocket. What had he just gotten his father involved in?

Chapter Thirteen

Fifer and Oscar met with Orville at his store later that afternoon, and she toured the older man's business. His pride in the ancient store shown on him like a badge of honor. He invited her to church and Sunday lunch the coming weekend. She said no the first four times, but the man was more stubborn than Oscar, even more stubborn than she was. She finally agreed to the lunch but managed to get out of the church service.

"Don't you believe in God?" Orville asked as they looked through a dusty box of vinyl records.

"I do." Fifer picked up a Bee Gees album. Barry Gibb with his two other brothers, she couldn't remember their names, strolled boldly toward whatever was in front of them. Her mother had loved the Bee Gees. She put the album down. "I may go to your church one day, but not yet."

"Well, I hope you'll give us a try before you get done with the theater and leave town." Orville picked up the Bee Gees album and slipped it back in the box between Conway Twitty and Kiss. "God would love to have you visit us, and so would I."

Would the rest of the people of Red Creek? Fifer followed Orville around his store, listening as he told tales of where he'd gotten this item or that. Oscar trailed along silently behind them. She was doing what her father insisted, connecting with the town, paving the way for him to send in his goons, and start his usual operation. She would not use church or God to do Louis McKenzie's dirty work. Her hell would be hot enough, no doubt, without piling that sin on top of it. "Hmm?" She looked at Orville, now standing in front of her at the counter. "I'm sorry. I got a little distracted by all of your things. What did you say?"

"I said have Oscar text you our address. Come on out about noon Sunday. Wear something comfortable, and bring a good appetite. My sister and daughter are the two best cooks in Red Creek." He looked from Fifer to Oscar, propping his body against the tall counter. "Boy, if you tell your momma I said that I'll have your hide."

Fifer laughed. "I'll do that." She looked at Oscar, his expression calm, almost bored. He didn't have a clue what he had. What would it be like to hear a comment like that from your father, and it not affect you, not send dread down your spine? She reached her hand across the counter. "I've enjoyed the tour, Mr. Robinson, and I look forward to meeting the rest of Oscar's family this weekend."

Orville wiped his hand on his shirtfront and shook Fifer's. "I promise you. They are even more excited about meeting you." He looked over at Oscar. "Isn't that right, son?"

"No comment," Oscar said, rolling his eyes.

Friday morning, after Fifer brought coffee from the gas station to Oscar four days in a row, he decided it was time to introduce her to the place where most of the local folks got their morning caffeine. They'd left their duplex, getting into their vehicles that morning at the same time. "Follow me," he'd called to her as she'd slid behind the wheel.

He watched her smile at him across the small table of the Red Creek Pastry Shop. "The name is not very imaginative," she said, "but who cares when their pastries taste like this." She took a bite of the jelly filled doughnut and the strawberry filling oozed from the flaky crust. It plopped onto the paper plate below.

Oscar looked around the crowded room. "Yeah. It's like this every day except Sundays." The corner of his mouth tilted upward, and he pointed to Fifer's chin. "You have a little jelly there."

"Oh." Fifer dabbed her chin with a napkin. "Thanks. Are they closed on Sundays? I bet they could make a killing with the before church crowd."

"I'm sure they could." Oscar lifted his coffee cup from the table. "But the owners, Bob and Carol, go to our church. They know it's more important to give the day to God than to make the money."

"Give the day to God." Fifer looked past Oscar to the gray-haired man running the counter. "That's something you don't hear much anymore."

"Maybe not in Birmingham, but most of these folks believe in that sort of thing." Oscar watched with fascination as Fifer's tongue darted out and licked the sugary coating from her top lip, unable to pull his eyes away.

"I'm beginning to see that." Fifer looked at Oscar and smiled, her eyes sparkling. "I wasn't too happy that Bill insisted we spend time roaming the streets of Red Creek every day. I felt like it was a waste of our time." She reached her hand up and smoothed back her hair. "But I have decided he was right. People in this little town live by their own set of rules that seem to be better than the rest of the world's."

"I bet you'd be surprised at how similar we are to a lot of other small towns across the country," Oscar said, forcing his attention back to their conversation. "We're mostly decent, law-abiding folks just trying to live our lives the way God intended. Christian folks doing their best to please their creator."

"Possibly." Fifer sipped her coffee. "Either way, I'm now positive we need to make sure the entertainment and the aesthetics of the dinner theater match the town's opinion of what is good for its people." She took another bite of her doughnut and lifted her eyes upward. Her lips wrapped around the pastry, then her eyelids fluttered close, the look on her face one of pure joy.

Throughout their conversation, Oscar had to make himself concentrate. Her tongue would dart out and lick the glossy red jelly from her lips, or her hand would flitter to her collar bone or touch her cheek, and her hair. What would it be like to pull those blasted pins from that knot and let the curls fall free like they should?

She was changing, right before his eyes, and it was going to be his undoing. It had only been two weeks of being in her company, and he was falling for her. True, except for his time on Red Creek during the weekends, they had spent every waking minute together. Even on the banks of Red Creek, his place, his special oasis, she'd invaded. Not in bodily form, but definitely in his thoughts. He'd let a really nice bass get away last weekend because of his daydreaming. Then he'd nearly burned his hand at the campfire because he'd been imagining how she'd looked that night in the moonlight. Wondering what she would look like on the creek bank under the stars—beside him.

"Mr. Robinson said your mother was a singer back in the day?"

Oscar blinked and looked at Fifer. "She was. She still is, I guess. She sings at Olivia's restaurant and the Blue Hotel from time to time."

"What's her name? Would I recognize her?"

"Lucy Robinson." Oscar leaned back in the little wooden chair and crossed his arms over his chest. "She wasn't huge, like Dolly Parton or Reba, but she was sort of big for a while."

"Wait." Fifer set down her coffee cup and leaned forward. "Your mother is Lucy Robinson? Alabama's darling?"

"Yep."

"Why in the world didn't you tell me? Why didn't your father tell me?" Fifer's hand came up, and her fingers stroked her cheek. "She's famous, and she lives here in Red Creek?"

"She uh." Oscar pulled himself up straight in the chair. How did he explain this to her? He'd forgiven his mother for running away all those years ago to make a name for herself. It hadn't been easy, but with a lot of prayer and a lot of talking to his mother, he'd come to realize that she had changed. The breast cancer had led her to Christ and also led her back home.

Orville had asked Oscar to read the prodigal son parable in the Bible. Oscar had read it every single day for weeks when his mother moved back to town. He could practically quote it now. Finally, he'd let go of the anger and malice, and had accepted his mother's apology. Now they were building a new relationship. Forgiveness had been harder for him than it had for the rest of the family. He still had a little trouble talking about his mother leaving all those years ago. When people talked about his mother's career, the leaving always came up . . . eventually.

Oscar pulled in a breath of air and looked at Fifer, waiting for his answer. "She's my mother. I try not to think of all that other stuff about her that . . ."

Fifer's eyes narrowed. "You said she wasn't around when you were little." Her voice grew soft with contemplation. "The fame kept her away from you and your siblings, didn't it?"

"Sort of." Oscar ran his hand through his black hair, his own curls falling back into place. "She left my father, and he raised us kids. She just came back last year. They got remarried right after our house burned. That's why I'm living next door to you now."

Somehow, over the next hour, Oscar poured out his life story to Fifer, telling her about being the oldest to five younger siblings who all wanted their mother. About living with a father who had withdrawn from the joy of life, who struggled to keep everyone headed in the right direction. About an aunt who had given her life to her little brother and his kids instead of seeking a life of her own.

"No wonder you didn't say anything." Fifer reached across the table and squeezed Oscar's hand. "Her career sort of ruined her family's life."

Oscar swallowed. The warmth of Fifer's hand on his sent a tingle through his gut. "No, that's what I thought for a long, long time, but not anymore. I wouldn't give anything for my family or being raised by my father and Aunt Sadie. God worked it all out." Oscar looked down at her hand on top of his. He turned his hand over, and his calloused skin touched her smooth palm. His heart flipped. "I don't know why I'm dumping this on you. I've never told anybody about my life like I'm telling it to you."

Fifer's eyes pulled up from their hands to Oscar's face. "I'm glad you did."

"Would you do me a favor?" The words flowed from Oscar's mouth before he could stop them. Fifer nodded, not speaking. "When you come out to my parent's place Sunday, wear your hair down. For me."

Fifer pulled her hand back. *What was I thinking?* Oscar groaned inwardly. This was Fifer McKenzie, the woman he was supposed to cater to, the woman with a reputation for eating people alive. *I'm a dope.*

Oscar's blue eyes locked with Fifer's green eyes. Her hands slowly reached behind her head and pulled out the pins. A red flaming rope of hair fell across her shoulder, and she smiled. Oscar swallowed as her fingers moved through her hair, releasing it from the tight confines she put it in every day.

"It's going to be a hot mess in a matter of minutes," Fifer said, her eyes studying his face. "That's why I keep it pinned up. I can't control it any other way."

"It's pretty up." Oscar's eyes tore away from Fifer's and took in the river of flaming curls surrounding her. It took every bit of restraint to remember they were in the Red Creek pastry shop. The morning crowd had thinned, but there were still eyes taking them in right now. What would they think? Did he care? *No, I don't care one bit.* "Control is okay, but it's beautiful when you set it free."

Chapter Fourteen

Fifer's finger languidly twirled the loose curl hanging on her shoulder. She'd lost her mind. How else could she explain what was happening to her? She tucked her bare feet under her backside and relaxed against her couch. The gauzy curtains behind where she sat covered the living room window and let her look into her front yard without it being too obvious that she was spying on her neighbor. Her cheeks flushed just thinking about how she had brazenly taken her hair down in the doughnut shop. How Oscar had not been able to take his eyes off of her, how he had called her beautiful.

Oscar's door opened and shut, and she slipped down lower below the back of the couch. She grabbed a throw pillow and hugged it to her chest. Yeah, she was spying. No need to deny it. Festus shot across the yard to Oscar's truck, lifted his leg on the tire, then darted back out of sight toward Oscar's porch. She strained her ears but couldn't make out what Oscar was saying to the animal.

A couple of seconds later, Oscar in cargo shorts, a tee-shirt and tennis shoes, a duffle bag slung over his shoulder, walked across the lawn to his truck. He was definitely good looking in his dress clothes. His tan skin against his starchy white shirt was an eye catcher. He had three ties he rotated wearing to work. She shouldn't notice that, but he had a habit of tugging at the tie's knot when she got under his skin. This afternoon, in his casual clothes, he was every bit as handsome. He slung the duffle bag into the back of the truck and opened the cab door. His dark five-o'clock shadow fit the everyday man look he was sporting right now. But where was he going? If she got in her car she could follow him. Of course, that would be wrong and intrusive, but . . . .

After Oscar's truck backed out of the drive and started down the road, Fifer tossed aside the throw pillow and sprang up, grabbing her purse from the coffee table. She slipped her feet into the flip-flops near the front door and headed out. *You really have lost your ever-loving mind, Fifer McKenzie.* She hopped in her car and backed out of the driveway. Had she locked the front door? The crime rate was practically nonexistent in Red Creek, and she wouldn't be gone long. It would be okay.

She gave the car a little more gas as she headed out of town. The back of Oscar's truck came into view as she rounded a curve. She eased back. So far, she had not seen any other Miatas in Red Creek. If he saw her car she was busted. They continued out of town onto a double lane road toward the country. Fifer reached into her bag and put on her shades. A lot of good that would do if he saw her, but at least she felt a little more incognito.

Oscar's truck disappeared around a curve and she sped up again, passing more cow fields and trees now than houses. A couple of seconds later, she came out of the curve and passed Oscar's truck pulled to the side of the road with the window rolled down. He waved as she sped by, Festus looking out the window with him like they were just hanging out, having a leisurely break on their way to wherever he was going.

She jerked her head back toward the road, her knuckles gripping the steering wheel like a vise. Now what? She watched in her rearview mirror as his truck pulled behind her. She could keep going—see how far he would follow her, but he would follow her all the way to the coast. There was no doubt about that.

A gravel drive leading to a fenced in cow field came into view ahead. Might as well get this over with. She could deny she was following him, but he knew she was. How would he respond? She pushed her hair back where it had fallen over her shoulder. It was strange how a thing like a hair style could make her feel confident, or in this case, vulnerable.

She eased her little car onto the drive and Oscar pulled in right behind her, his tires crunching in the loose gravel. She got out and leaned against the closed door, waiting for him to come to her.

"Hey," he said, mirth dripping from his tone. He looked even more handsome when he was relaxed, like he obviously was now. He took his time walking to where she waited.

"Hello." She raised her chin. "This weather is perfect for taking an afternoon drive." Oscar stepped directly in front of her. A cow off in the field bellowed, and Fifer turned her head. She could feel Oscar's eyes not looking away. He continued to stare at her, not in the least bit of a hurry to get to wherever he was going. She squeezed her hands together at her side to keep from fidgeting with her hair.

"You going to the coast for the weekend?" he asked.

"Maybe." Festus barked from the nearby truck cab, and she turned to look. She grinned at the dog sitting in the driver's seat, paws on the steering wheel.

This time, Oscar followed her gaze. "He's going to jump

out the window in a second, then I'll have to chase him down."

"Well, don't let me keep you." Fifer looked back at Oscar. "I know you have some sort of standing appointment on the weekends."

Oscar stepped closer, and the smell of soap wafted Fifer's nostrils. He reached up and lifted her shades. "I like your eyes," he said. "They're green."

"That's what they tell me," she whispered. He was so close. She leaned forward.

Oscar leaned down. Without her heels on, he was a few inches taller than her. His lips pressed against hers, and an electric bolt shot all the way down to her manicured toenails. The scruff of whiskers raked against her skin, and she breathed in his clean scent. Her eyes closed. Warmth poured from his lips and trickled down her middle. A ripple from somewhere inside her rose up with a warmth of its own. She reached up and wrapped her arms around his neck, her fingers finding his hair. The cows, the vehicles going up and down the nearby road, even Festus, floated out of her mind. She pulled closer, drinking in every part of him he was giving her.

Oscar pulled away, and she sucked in a gulp of air. "I was following you," she blurted out. "I know it's unprofessional and intrusive. I didn't think. I just climbed in the car and took off after you."

"I like it."

Oscar's deep voice rumbled around her. She wished he would lean down again, but he didn't. She reached up to touch his face, then lowered her hand. Her brow furrowed. "Like what?"

"You . . . not thinking, just doing. Following me." He stepped back and held up her shades, still in his hand. "You want to see where I go every weekend?"

"I don't want to intrude." She looked at his raised

eyebrows and rolled her eyes. "Okay. Yes. I'm dying to know where you disappear to on the weekends. Are you a baby-daddy or something and have to go see your kid?"

"If I was, what would you think?"

Fifer pressed her lips together. "That you are a decent father, I guess." She shrugged her shoulders. "Is that it?"

"No." Oscar handed her the shades. "Get in your car and follow me."

Fifer frowned as he walked back to the truck. The kiss. Weren't they going to say something about the kiss? She climbed into her car. Oh, they would. As soon as they got to wherever it was Oscar was leading her, she definitely wanted to talk about that kiss.

"Okay, now what?" Oscar backed out of the gravel drive. He glanced over at Festus as he turned onto the road. "I kissed her. I ogled her with my eyes this morning in the doughnut shop, and then I kissed her this evening." Festus leaned over and licked the right side of Oscar's face. "I know, I know." Oscar shoved Festus away and wiped the wetness from his cheek. "You slobber over me all the time, but this is different. You're my dog. She's my . . . ." Oscar raked his fingers through his hair. "She's my coworker."

He looked in the rearview mirror at her little red car. He was attracted, very attracted to Fifer McKenzie. She was attracted to him too. The way she let her hair down this morn-ing, the way she followed him, the way she responded to his kiss, she had to be attracted. The problem was, what would he do with that attraction? She was leaving when this project was over.

There was also the problem of who she was. Odi had emailed him some things he'd dug up on Fifer's father, and none of it was pretty. The man had been accused of several shady things over the years, including dabbling in drug dealing and illegal gambling. Earlier that afternoon, Oscar had gone to Bill Crestfield with his questions about Louis McKenzie. Bill tried to make light of Oscar's concerns.

"The man has never been found guilty of anything, Oscar." Bill had fumbled with some papers on his desk, clearly uncomfortable with being questioned about his business decisions. "You have nothing to worry about. This is a solid contractual agreement."

"But why do business with a man like that in the first place, Mr. Crestfield?" Oscar had refused to be put off by his boss. He'd worked with him long enough to know the man was hiding something. "Why didn't you bring in partners who didn't have such a questionable reputation? People you could trust one hundred percent?"

"I had to buy quickly." Bill Crestfield's words came out in a rush as he raised his voice. "If I'd taken the time to gather enough investors to do the project, the owners would have sold the property to someone else." He flopped back in his chair, his voice dropping to its normal octave. "McKenzie had the money to invest, so I took him up on his offer."

"What's in it for him?" Oscar ignored the dramatics of his boss. He was a great salesman, while his brother Grant had more of a head for the business side of things. Together through the years, they had made some sound investments in real estate, the stock market, and other ventures. They weren't on the same level as Gordon Blue, the hotel owner and wealthiest man in the state, but they were solid businessmen. At least they always had been before. "Why would

Louis McKenzie want to invest in our little town?" Oscar asked.

"We're growing." Bill Crestfield sat forward again. "He's getting in on the ground level. Blue's hotel and your sister's restaurant are pulling in more tourism as people travel to the coastline. In a few more years, Red Creek will be a vacation spot all on its own." Oscar had left the office with more doubts than when he went in.

Oscar slowed his truck and turned down the gravel road. That white truck was at Aunt Sadie's again. Who was that guy? She hadn't brought him to church or over to lunch on Sunday, but he'd noticed the man's truck there for the past three weekends. He waved at his aunt standing on her front porch, watching him and the little red car as they passed. She didn't like anyone asking her personal questions, but he was certain she wouldn't have any qualms about quizzing him down about the woman in the car following him to the creek bank.

His truck turned again on the narrow dirt road leading to his land, then slowed to a crawl. Fifer would have to creep along through the ruts and holes in her low riding car, and he didn't want to leave her behind. A majestic buck with a huge rack froze at the edge of the tree line then darted out of sight as their vehicles crept past. Oscar looked in his rear-view mirror. Fifer's head was turned to the side watching where the animal had disappeared.

No, he wasn't a baby-daddy. He just had a hair-brained idea about turning his love of fishing and his love of Red Creek into a business. At least he hadn't spilled his guts about that to her. A woman like Fifer wouldn't understand leaving a successful and secure career to chase a pipe dream. Although she had seemed to respect his father for doing what he loved.

Oscar pulled his truck to its usual spot and opened the door.

Festus jumped out, but instead of bounding off into the woods in his usual habit, he ran over to Fifer's car and waited while she got out. She squatted beside him and scratched his neck, then nuzzled his nose. How could this woman in the yoga pants, oversized sweatshirt, and flip-flops be the same woman he'd been dealing with for the past three weeks? Maybe she'd been this way all along and he'd been too aggravated with her to see it. He certainly saw her now, and he liked what he saw. He just didn't know what to do about it.

Chapter Fifteen

Fifer looked at Oscar's shadowy figure walking through the moonlight. She should have left hours ago. He came to this place to unwind, sort of like her yoga time. She wouldn't appreciate someone pushing into her exercise ritual and making themselves at home. As a matter of fact, she had kind of laid down the law about the backyard and Festus for that very reason. Yet—here she was. And there he was. Bringing cans of Beanie Weenies from the back of his truck for their dinner.

"I'm sorry." Fifer eased over on the horse blanket Oscar had laid out for her to sit on. She watched him pick up his 'poking stick' and stir the small fire in front of them.

"For what?" Oscar popped the four little cans of beans and franks and poured them in his cast-iron skillet.

"For intruding." Fifer watched him hold the skillet over the coals and tiny flames. "This is your place, and I barged in."

"You're forgiven." Oscar shook the skillet, then reached into his cargo shorts, and pulled out a fork. "You weren't thinking, remember?"

"Yeah." Fifer hugged her knees up to her chest. "This

morning, and then that kiss." She threw a wad of hair away from her face. "I'm not that type of woman."

"I'm not that type of man."

"I mean." Fifer strained her eyes in the dim firelight, trying to see Oscar's expression. He slowly stirred the skillet, not looking her way. "I don't go from town to town and fall in love with every hunky guy I happen to work with."

Oscar's face turned toward her. His teeth appeared as a smile broke across his face. "I am sort of hunky, aren't I?"

"Oh, good grief."

"Hand me those bowls." Oscar pointed to a dollar store bag a few feet away.

Fifer stretched over and grabbed the bag. She fished out a couple of Styrofoam bowls, then tossed the bag back into the darkness. "What I'm trying to say is, I don't want you to get the wrong idea about me. What's happened since I've been here has been very unique." She passed the bowls to Oscar's outstretched hand. "At least it has been for me . . . in lots of ways."

Oscar stepped back from the fire. She watched his silhouette pour the food into the bowls and fish a second fork from his pocket. He stepped over to the blanket and handed her a bowl, then fished in another pocket on the side of the baggy cargo shorts, and pulled out a bottle of water. "It's not much, but I wasn't expecting company."

"Oscar." Fifer waited for Oscar to sit on the blanket beside her. "It's important to me that you understand this. What I'm feeling . . . the way I'm behaving . . . it's all new to me."

"It's new to me too." Oscar looked at the fire. "I haven't had feelings like this since I was in college." He scooped up a forkful of beans and put them in his mouth. "That was not like this either."

Fifer studied his face. He had a strong jaw. His skin was

tanned under the shadow of whiskers, and his lips weren't too full. "I don't do well in relationships," she said. He turned and looked at her, his blue eyes catching the firelight. "I haven't been in many, but I messed them up. I'm sort of." She paused and bit her lower lip. The last time she'd been this vulnerable with anybody, she'd ended up spending a weekend in outpatient rehab, and a couple of weeks practically living with her sponsor. That was seven years ago. "I'm sort of messed up, Oscar."

"We're all messed up in one way or another." Oscar set his bowl down. His hand brushed a curl away from her cheek. "That's life."

"But I'm messed up in a lot of ways. Really important ways." Her face leaned into his hand. "What I'm saying is, you may want to step away . . . from me. I'm not a good risk. We can stop this now. I can get in my car and leave. If you tell me to."

Oscar's finger trailed from Fifer's cheek to her lips. "Shh. Let's eat—enjoy each other's company, and not try to figure all of this out at once."

"I don't." Her lips trembled. She reached up and put her hand over his. "I don't sleep around. I don't want you to get the wrong idea."

Oscar pulled his hand down, his voice husky. "I don't either." He scooted back on the blanket. "Maybe you going home would be a good idea." He reached up again and touched a curl laying on her shoulder. "Not because I don't want you here, but because I want you here too much."

"I think you're right." Fifer bit down on her lip. "I'd better go."

"You can finish your dinner." Oscar's fingers went up to her jaw. "No need to leave hungry."

"No." Fifer swallowed. "I'd better go. Now." She stood and looked down at his upturned face. "While I still can."

⤞⤝

Oscar didn't stand. He didn't need to follow her. If he did, he would ask her to stay, and that was not the guy he wanted to be—not the guy he was. If he was going to pursue his feelings for her, and apparently he was, because every time he was around her, his voice of reason flew out the window. He wanted to do this the right and honorable way.

He picked up Fifer's abandoned bowl of beanie-weenies and lifted out the fork. He dumped her untouched meal into his bowl, then tossed her empty bowl into the fire. Earlier, after she had gotten out of her car and loved on Festus, she'd insisted on walking back up the dirt road to where they had seen the deer. "That buck is long gone." He'd tried to dissuade her from wasting her time looking for the animal, but she wasn't having it. She could soften her demeanor, but that hardheaded thing she had going on went to her core.

"I've never been out in a forest like this." She'd looked over her shoulder at him as she headed down the path, Festus at her side. "I want to look around. You don't have to come with me. I'm a big girl."

"We call it the woods." He'd jogged up to her side, squeezing in between her and his dog. "Forest is a word for story books and city people." She'd stuck her tongue out at him and kept walking. "I know you can handle yourself," he said, "but snakes love to crawl this time of year, and they are easily camouflaged by the leaves and dirt." That had stopped her in her tracks.

"I didn't think about snakes." She'd scanned the ground around her. "Is it safe to walk through here?"

"You'll be fine, but here." He'd stepped off the road and

picked up a stick about three feet long. "Take this poking stick."

Her lips twisted into a smirk. "Poking stick? You're making that up."

"That's what we've always called them at my house." He put the stick in her hand. "Poke around into the leaves as you walk along. That way, if a snake is down there, you'll know it before you step on it."

They'd walked down the road, Fifer poking the ground in front of her like a misguided hockey player. They made their way back to the camp just as the sun was setting. She'd pushed up her yoga pants and waded in the icy creek water while he built a fire. She hadn't questioned his motives for coming here, hadn't insinuated he was hiding from the world. Bringing her here hadn't been his idea, at least not initially, but it had been a good thing.

Oscar looked over his shoulder, searching through the darkness for her figure, missing her already. Her car lights should be coming on in a second. If he hurried, he could catch her before she left. Not for the reasons of before. He'd cooled down a little, and all of that was under control for now. He would just tell her bye. Tell her he was glad she came. Tell her . . .

A scream cut through the night. Oscar leapt to his feet. Barking drowned out his pounding heart, and his footsteps crashing against the ground as he raced toward the sound. Why hadn't he walked with her? She must have stepped on a snake. *Stupid, stupid, stupid man! You should have taken better care of her.*

A light flashed up from the ground near Fifer's car, and Oscar hurried to it. "What happened?" He squatted beside her and looked at her foot where her cell phone light was pointing. Blood, bright red, and a lot of it, ran from the arch of her foot. "That's not good."

"I stepped on something. Glass, I guess." Fifer's voice was shaky, but surprisingly calm. "It's pretty deep, I think."

"I think so too." Oscar pushed Festus away from Fifer's foot. He peeled off his tee-shirt and shoved it onto her free-flowing wound. "Can you hold that on there while I take you to the truck?"

"Yeah." She winced as he pushed the cloth deep into the cut. "I think so."

"Good." He scooped her up in his arms, and she let out a little moan. "Sorry. We've got to get you to the hospital. You need stitches."

Fifer laid her head on his chest, not answering. He ran the few feet to his truck and opened the passenger's door, trying not to jostle her around too much. He grabbed a spare tee-shirt he kept in the cab while Festus hopped into the back seat. "Are you still okay?" He looked over at Fifer in the glaring overhead truck light. She was as pale as a ghost. The tee-shirt on her foot was wet with blood. He hurried around to his side of the truck and slid behind the wheel. He pushed the button on the light to make it stay on after he closed the door. If she passed out while he was driving, he wanted to see it.

"I'm fine." Fifer leaned back against the passenger's door, one knee bent, the other leg straight with her injured foot stretched across the seat.

Oscar gently lifted her foot and cradled it on his thigh. He slammed the truck door and started out of the woods. "I'll have you in the emergency room in a few minutes." He reached down with one hand and applied more pressure to the cut. Fifer pushed her head back and drew in a sharp breath through her teeth. "I'm sorry," he said, "but it's bleeding pretty badly. They will give you something for the pain as soon as we get there."

Fifer's head jerked up. Her red hair flamed against her

white skin, now damp with perspiration. "No." Her eyes stretched wide. "No pain medicine, Oscar."

Oscar turned onto the main road heading into Red Creek and punched the accelerator. "Fifer, you're bleeding like a stuck pig. I know how tough you are, but everybody needs something for pain when they get stitches, and believe me, you're gonna need stitches."

Fifer leaned forward and grabbed Oscar's hand, holding the tee-shirt against her foot, her fingernails cutting into his flesh. "No pain medicine, Oscar. I mean it. Even if I pass out, you have to promise me you won't let them give me anything for pain."

"Fifer."

"Promise me."

Oscar's eyes darted from Fifer's panicked face to her hand with the death grip on his arm, then back to the road. "Okay. I promise." Her grip on his arm relaxed as he took the curve into town at breakneck speed. Festus flopped against the side of the truck, then righted himself. Oscar turned and looked at her face. Her eyes were closed, and her head was laying back against the passenger's door. Had she fainted? "Fifer?"

"Yeah." Only her lips moved.

"It's going to be alright. I'm going to take care of you."

"No pain meds, Oscar," she whispered. "Please."

The truck slowed, and he turned into the emergency room parking lot. "No pain meds." He reached out and ran his hand along the side of her face. "No pain meds."

Chapter Sixteen

Fifer glared at the bright lights in the treatment room of the ER. After seeing the bloody rag on her foot that had been Oscar's tee-shirt only a short while ago, the clerk in the waiting area called a nurse to take her straight back. The nurse had attempted to make Oscar stay in the waiting area, but he nor Fifer were having it. "If he can't come with me, I'm not going," she said, staring the nurse in the eye. Despite the electrical pain in her foot and feeling like she'd black out if she tried to stand on her own, Fifer had managed an authoritative scowl that even her father would have admired.

The doctor and her nurse looked at the wound, offered IV pain meds, then rinsed and held pressure on Fifer's bloody foot, and offered IV pain meds a second time. The doctor stepped out of the room and took Oscar with her. Fifer watched the nurse open up some kind of suture kit while they waited for the doctor to return.

"Miss McKenzie." The doctor stepped back into the room, Oscar right behind her. "I've tried to convince your friend that this will go a whole lot easier if you would let us slip in an IV and give you something to ease the pain." The doctor looked over her shoulder at Oscar, glaring at her, his feet apart, and his arms crossed on his chest like some kind of Navy SEAL boy scout. At least he was taking his promise seriously. The doctor turned back to Fifer. "But since I'm getting nowhere with either of you, this is what we will do. I'm going to numb your foot a little with lidocaine."

Fifer opened her mouth to object, but the doctor held up her hand. "Listen to me before you say anything. Lidocaine is like the medicine you rub on a baby's gums when they're teething. It will not affect you systemically and trigger whatever problem you have with pain medication." The doctor crossed her arms over her chest and glowered down at Fifer. "I will not have you jumping off the cot while I'm attempting to sew up your foot. You have to let me numb the area."

Fifer looked from the frowning doctor to Oscar. His eyes narrowed a hairsbreadth. She hadn't prayed in a long time. That night in her backyard hadn't really counted. *Lord, don't let me slip into the pit. Not now. Please, God.* "Okay." Fifer sucked in a deep breath. "Let's get this over with."

An hour later, the doctor finished sewing up and bandaging her foot. Her arm was sore from the tetanus shot, but her head was clear. The nurse had made her give a urine sample, then had drawn a couple of tubes of blood. Fifer wasn't sure what that was about, but imagined the doctor suspected her addiction problem. That was fine. Let them check her blood, urine, and whatever else. She was clean as a whistle and planned on staying that way. Poor Oscar. He had insisted on staying in the room for the entire procedure, blocking her view from where the doctor was sewing her foot. His skin had turned a little green during the ordeal, but he had been a real trooper.

The nurse pushed Fifer's wheelchair through the emergency room's sliding glass doors where Oscar stood, the passenger door to his truck open. Festus barked from the back seat. Poor Festus. She'd forgotten he was along for the ride.

Oscar helped her into the truck, and she clamped her teeth together. Showing signs of pain would bring on an argument, and she was too tired to argue.

"Does it hurt?" Oscar slid behind the steering wheel and looked at Fifer's clenched jaw.

"Nothing I can't handle." Festus leaned across the seat and nuzzled Fifer's head. She leaned into his warmth. The hug, the unconditional love, felt fantastic at that moment.

"I know it hurts." Oscar pulled to the edge of the parking lot and stopped. He tipped forward so he could see Fifer's face around his dog. "Tell me what I can do to help."

Fifer pushed the tears back. Not tears of pain. The throb was beating like a bass drum in her foot, but she was handling that. The monster was on her tail, head and shoulders out of the pit, farther than he'd been out in years. "I want to go home."

"You sure that's it?" Oscar reached over and wiped away a tear escaping down her cheek. "It's killing me to see you in pain and not being able to help."

She blinked back the tears, swallowed down her weakness. She'd made it through getting her foot sewed up. That was the easy part. She looked over at Oscar, his face so intense with concern for her. Had anyone ever looked at her like that? Really cared like that? She sat up straighter and forced her lips into a smile. "It's not that bad. I just want to go home and get some sleep." Festus licked her cheek again. "You know what? I'm sort of hungry."

"What do you want?" Oscar looked at the clock on the truck dash. "It's after ten. Olivia's place is closed, but they're still there cleaning and stuff. I can get her to hook us up with something."

"No." Fifer bit her lip. *He needs to make things better.* "I think ice cream. Is there a drugstore or some place around to get ice cream?"

"Ice cream it is."

Oscar pulled out of the parking lot, focused on the mission Fifer had given him. He ran through the list of stores around them, discarding the ones that would already be closed. Fifer eased her head back against the seat and closed her eyes as he talked. Is this what having a relationship with Oscar Robinson would be like? Her falling, and him picking her up? Part of her longed for that security, knowing that his arms would be there, keep her from going into the pit.

She felt the truck slow and turn. Oscar's hand cupped her cheek, and she opened her eyes. "Are we home?"

"No. I'm running in to get the ice cream. Do you need anything else?"

"No," she whispered. She reached her hand up and covered his. "I'm good."

"I'll be right back."

She watched him hurry from the truck and jog across the lot to the gas station/convenience store. *I can't do this to him.* More tears slid down her face. If she let him in like she was doing, her problem . . . her monster . . . would become his. He would figure it out. He probably already had. Her heart squeezed. If he had already figured it out and he was still around, wasn't that a good thing? *No. He doesn't know what it's like. What if I fall into the pit? What if he sees me in a messed- up stupor and doesn't want me?*

The back of Fifer's hand slashed across her face, taking away her tears and her vulnerability. She'd give herself tonight. She needed him close tonight. Needed his strength. But tomorrow the wall had to go up. *You could lean on God instead. He's held you up before.* Fifer pushed the thought to the back of her mind. Leaning was weakness. Weakness was why she was in this mess. Tomorrow she'd be stronger, stop letting her feelings control her like they had been more and more ever since she moved into Red Creek. She reached back and pulled Festus close to her chest. After tonight, she'd set Oscar free. He deserved that.

❦

"Fifer!" The following morning Oscar banged on her front door with the side of his fist. "What's going on?" He stepped over to the living room window and peered through the gauzy curtains. The lights were on. The pillow and blanket he'd brought down for her the night before lay crumpled up on the couch where she'd slept. Maybe she'd slipped in the bathroom and knocked herself out.

"Fifer!" Oscar's voiced bellowed through his chest, loud enough to wake everybody up and down the street. "Fifer, if I don't hear anything, I'm coming in." Could he break down the front door? He rolled his shoulders. He could sure try.

"Hold on." Fifer's solemn voice sounded from the other side of the door. Thank goodness.

"Good morning." Oscar leaned in through the doorframe, his lips missing her cheek as she dodged to the side. His eyebrows drew together, and he straightened, taking in her appearance. Her hair was falling around her in a gloriously tangled mess. She had on different yoga pants, red ones, and a black over-sized sweatshirt. Her good foot was in one of the running shoes he saw her wear when she was in the backyard most evenings, but her bandaged foot was in a grey slipper. His eyes rose to her face, and her eyes darted away from his. The soft smile that had been so prevalent for the past few days was gone. "I'm going to Red Creek to get your car. I thought you might want to ride along."

"No, thank you." Fifer's voice was firm, businesslike.

"Okay." Oscar drug out the word and tilted his head to the side. "Everything alright?"

"Everything is fine." Fifer's chin lifted, and her eyes connected with his. "There is one thing. Please don't bang on my door like that again. If I want to see you, I'll answer. If I don't, please don't embarrass yourself or me by making a scene."

"Fifer?" Oscar stepped forward but stopped when she put her hand on his chest.

"Don't, Oscar." She swallowed, her eyes cutting to the left. "Just . . . do as I ask. Please."

Oscar stepped back, and her hand dropped from his chest to her side. "If that's what you want." He searched her face.

"It is."

"Okay." He tilted his chin down, and his eyes narrowed. "I'll be back with your car in a little while."

"Thank you."

The door shut in front of him. He stood there, staring, the conversation playing over in his head. What had he done? Why was she pushing him away? He turned and walked to his truck. His plan had been to pick up her car from the creek bank, then see if she wanted to go to church with him before they went to lunch at his parent's house. They would go to church in her little toy car. It didn't matter who saw him in it or what they said. Or at least it hadn't mattered a few minutes ago.

Oscar drove out to Red Creek and pulled his truck into its usual parking spot. He walked over to where Fifer's car waited and searched the ground. A jagged piece of glass stained with blood lay near where he'd found her the night before. For years, before his father officially deeded him the land, local teens came to this section of the creek to swim during the summer. It was deep enough to dive and rough house in, unlike a lot of other areas along the water way. A rope tied to a limb hanging over the opposite bank a few yards down from his campsite was a favorite spot for swinging into the water. All the Robinson kids had done tricks off that swing before, along with most of the inhabitants of Red Creek.

He picked up the glass and scanned the ground around him. He didn't see anymore, but he needed to come out and really go over the place. He hadn't noticed this chunk of glass, and look what had happened. He placed the glass in the back of his truck and walked to the little car. He climbed into the seat. Fifer was tall, so he wasn't bent like a pretzel, but he let the seat back the rest of the way. Her purse lay in the passenger's seat. He didn't need to fish out the key, it just had to be near the ignition.

Oscar started the car and headed down the dirt road. She was in pain. She had to be. He needed to give her a few days to heel, back away, and give her space. He pulled onto the paved road and shifted the car into second, then third, enjoying driving a standard. She wouldn't take pain medicine, almost like she had a phobia about it. Odi had told Oscar that Fifer's father had been accused of being involved in drug dealing. Did that have something to do with it? If so, she was acting pretty irrational, and that didn't fit with who Fifer was. She seemed to be very methodical in her decision making, sort of like he was.

Did someone she love have a drug problem? She said her mother died when she was eighteen. If her mother was an addict, especially if she died from some kind of overdose, that could cause Fifer to fear taking pain medication. Especially if she was scared the problem was inherited. That had to be it.

He pulled the car into Fifer's drive as her cell phone started ringing. He lifted her purse and looked at the phone sitting at the top of her things. Louis McKenzie's face appeared on the screen with the word Father across the bottom. Why was this man investing in a dinky little theater in Red Creek? He got out of the car with Fifer's purse and phone in hand. The phone stopped ringing as he reached the front door. He raised his hand to knock, but Fifer opened the door first. "Here you go."

"Thank you."

"If you need me, you have my number."

"I'm fine." Fifer stared at him for a few seconds, face somber, then shut the door.

Oscar walked down her steps, then up his. He would give her space, but he wouldn't give up on her. He hadn't felt this way about anyone before. When he heard her scream last night, his heart had ripped. He was falling for her and didn't want to stop. He would prefer a whirlwind, sky dive type of fall, but if she wanted a slow, drippy molasses fall, he would do that. Whatever was needed to have her.

He hurried up the stairs to get ready for church. *Lord, help her. I don't know where she is with You, God, but please help her get through all of this. She needs You. I don't know if she knows it, but I do, and You do. Help her lean on You to heal. Help me be what I need to be for her.*

Chapter Seventeen

Long didn't even begin to describe her week. Fifer sat on the mat in her living room, eyes closed, breathing in and out. She'd planned to work Monday morning, business as usual, but driving a stick shift with a sliced foot didn't work too well. Since her right foot couldn't handle the pressure, she tried clutching the stupid sports car with her left foot. She couldn't even back out of the drive without the thing revving like it was in the Indy 500 or jumping like a thoroughbred racehorse. She'd had the brains to wait until Oscar had already left for work before attempting the feat, so at least he didn't see her humiliate herself and have to hobble back inside the house.

Later that morning, she'd asked the mailman if Red Creek had Uber. He'd asked if that was a giant boiled peanut. When she hadn't laughed at his little joke, he'd said no, and they didn't have a taxi service either. It had probably been for the best that she stayed at home that first day.

One of the reasons for her mood wasn't only her foot, but also her lack of sleep. The dream, the one with the snake and mud, had returned, waking her every night. She was snapping at the stove, the television, the stairs, her own body. Heaven knows she would have bitten the heads off actual people. She'd ended up calling Bill Crestfield and telling him she would be working from home for a couple of days.

"My niece saw you going into the hospital. She said you were cut so bad that you left a trail of blood across the ER waiting room." Bill's sympathetic voice grated on Fifer's nerves. "She told me about your foot. You take all the time you need, Fifer. Oscar will keep things going until you get back."

"It isn't that bad." Had she left a trail of blood like Bill said? No, the woman, whoever she was, had to be exaggerating. "Call me with any questions, and if anything needs signing, email it. I have my laptop. We will stay on schedule with everything, and I should be back in the office on Wednesday at the latest."

That afternoon, a bouquet of flowers arrived at her door from the Crestfield brothers. She'd cried—actually cried over the gesture. When she'd talked to her father Monday afternoon, and he discovered she hadn't been in the office because of the injury, all he'd done was threaten to send a goon to Red Creek if she got off schedule.

She'd gone through yoga without many problems, adapting the poses to keep the weight off her foot. By Wednesday, the swelling was going down and she could almost get a shoe on. Grant Crestfield had picked her up for work that morning. He was a lot more tactful than his brother and hadn't asked why she didn't ride in with Oscar. Grant was always in the background when Bill was around, but she had a feeling that he was the backbone of the business. Guilt washed over her. He would suffer from her father's tactics the most out of the two men. He truly cared about this business beyond it being a paycheck.

What could she do? Her father held her in his power. She'd tried to find a way out of his hold over her before. He held her secret in his hand. Two or three times over the past decade, she'd tried to sneak around and find out more information about what happened that night all those years ago, fill in the gaps that she couldn't remember. Every single time, her father had discovered what she was doing. Every single time, he reminded her that her future was in his hands and his alone and snooping in the past would only cause her more trouble.

Working until lunch, then coming home to prop up her confounded foot, had been the schedule for the last three days. She had avoided Oscar rather easily at work. She'd stayed in her office, and he hadn't attempted to come in to check on her. At home, she'd been the one looking for him. In secret, of course.

When his back door would open and close, she would hobble to the kitchen, stand in the shadows, and watch. She did the same with the front door, and it was almost like seeing two different men. The front door workday Oscar walked out with his suit on, long strides, focused on whatever job he needed to get done. Backdoor Oscar had at least lost the coat and tie, was usually in sweats and a tee-shirt. He would step out, sometimes stretch and look at the sky, sometimes squat and pet Festus, sometimes toss a ball, or even lay in the grass and let the dog climb on top of him. Backdoor spying made her heart ache, but she couldn't stop. Needing to see Oscar had turned into a craving. It was just as strong as the old one— and a lot more constant.

How will I ever push these feelings down? How will I control this thing I have for Oscar and stay out of the pit? She watched Festus run across the backyard, trot onto the little patio next door, then disappear into the house in front of Oscar. She turned and laid her shoulders against her kitchen wall. *God, I need help. I know I've had a sort of take You as I need You attitude. I need You now, God. I can't keep this up.*

Fifer looked down at her foot. She hadn't tried to drive since Monday. She walked as fast as she could manage through the little house, picking up her purse, not thinking. Thinking hurt too much. She sat on the couch and waited; her left leg bouncing with anticipation. A few minutes later, right on schedule, Oscar and Festus headed out their front door and drove away. He would be gone all weekend. She would be alone. Really alone.

She stood with her purse and hurried to her car. Shifting wasn't fun, but she managed it by having her toes bear all the weight, not letting the stitched area from the ball of her foot along the arch touch the clutch pad. The convenience store was just a few blocks away. She slipped on her shades and walked in—straight to the aisle she had, until this second, avoided like the plague in every store she'd entered for the past ten years. One bottle. I can make it last tonight and tomorrow, sleep it off Sunday, and be back at work on Monday. Sleep without the dreams. That's all I need. Lies, of course, but they sounded good enough.

She made it back home and sat on the couch, foot throbbing like nobody's business. The bottle set on the coffee table in front of her for ten long minutes. She reached out and wrapped her fingers around the neck. "It's the stress of this stupid foot." She peeled the wrapper off the cap. "I'll get through the weekend, and this will be it," she whispered. She tossed the bottle top on the couch beside her and turned the bottle up, not bothering to sip. It had been a long time. The burning trail from her lips to her gut almost felt good. "Nobody will know." She hugged the bottle to her chest. "Just for the weekend."

Sunday afternoon, Oscar leaned forward on the sofa in his parent's living room. His siblings had finally left, giving him the opportunity to talk with his father alone. He had considered talking to Owen about all the stuff going on in his life with Fifer, but Owen didn't quite get the concept of "this is between me and you only." He wouldn't intentionally tell anyone a secret, but Owen's brain had a tendency to hop from one topic to another. Things often passed between his brother's lips before his mind realized what direction his words were going in.

"Dad." Oscar looked at his father tuning the mandolin laying across his lap. "What would make a woman, any person, really, refuse to take something for pain?" His lips pushed into a flat line. "Not just minor pain, but genuine pain."

"You're talking about Fifer?" Orville looked up from the mandolin. "And her cut?"

"Yes, sir." Oscar pulled in a frustrated breath. "She was almost like a raccoon in a cage on the way to the hospital, and not any better once we got there. She wouldn't listen to reason." His mother walked into the room and handed Oscar a glass of tea. "Thank you." He took the tea glass and continued to look at his father.

"Do I need to leave and give you two some alone time?" Lucy asked.

"No." Oscar set the glass on a coaster on the coffee table in front of him. "I'm talking to Dad about Fifer." He watched his mother settle into the love seat beside his father. "But I do want this kept between us."

"Of course." Lucy Robinson tucked her bare feet under her thighs. "What did you do when she was like that?"

Oscar puffed his cheeks out and blew out a frustrated puff of air. "I promised to make sure she didn't get any pain meds. That's the only thing that halfway calmed her down. I tell you what." He leaned back on the couch and stretched his arms wide across the cushions. "That woman is tough as nails. The cut was deep and gushing blood. The doctor dug around in the wound to clean it, then stuck needles in her foot to numb it up before she stitched it closed. Fifer made a few faces, but she took it a lot better than I would have. I almost threw up just watching them."

"She's not a coward then." Orville picked up his tea glass from the end table beside the love seat and took a sip. "But it sure sounds like fear was driving her thinking about the pain medicine."

"It definitely was." Oscar pulled his arms in. "She told me her mother died when she was a teenager. The only thing I can figure is something might have happened to her mother, and she developed some kind of phobia because of it."

"That's possible." Lucy ran her finger around the edge of her tea glass, then looked up at Oscar. "Where is this woman at with the Lord?"

"I'm." Oscar leaned forward again, fidgeting through all the thoughts running around in his head. "Not sure. I've invited her to church, and dad has too, but she puts us off." He picked up his own tea glass, not that he was thirsty. He just needed something to occupy his hands and pull his attention away from his parents' scrutiny. He took a sip and set the glass down. "Why?"

"You're spending a lot of time with this woman, Oscar." Orville's lips turned up in a warm smile. "We can see you have some very strong feelings for her."

"I." Oscar wanted to stop their assumptions, deny his feelings for Fifer were growing, but he couldn't. "I enjoy her company. Even when we're fussing like cats and dogs, I still want to be around her."

Orville's smile stretched a little wider, and he reached beside him and patted Lucy on the knee. "I understand that feeling."

"I do too." Lucy leaned in and pecked Orville on the cheek. "That's why I asked my question. You may be right about Fifer having a phobia where pain medications are concerned, but it may be a lot more than that. But I guess I'm more concerned with how her problems." Lucy stopped and rolled her lips in. Her eyes searched the room and finally settled on Oscar. "I'm worried that you are falling for this woman and she is going to draw you away from God if she is lost." Lucy stopped again and looked at Orville for help with her thoughts.

"Son." Orville's face sobered. "Being friends with Fifer is one thing. She's a nice woman, as far as I can tell, but you need to guard your heart. Find out where she is with the Lord. You don't want to let yourself fall in love with a woman who isn't saved."

"Love?" Oscar snorted. "You're jumping the gun a little there, Dad." Oscar's eyes darted from his father to his mother, both staring at him, compassion in their eyes. "I like her." A lot. "We are friends, that's all." The words sounded false in Oscar's ears, but he hadn't come here to talk about his love life with his parents.

"In that case." Lucy's slim fingers tugged her earlobe. "You need to talk to her. Being scared of taking narcotics might be a sign of her having a problem, like an addiction."

"No." Oscar rubbed his hand across his chin. "I don't think so. She hasn't ever looked drunk or messed up or anything. Ever, and I see her at all times of the day."

"That could mean that she's got it under control, which is a hard thing to do." Lucy's eyes found Oscar's and held his gaze. "Son, just remember that when two people love each—"

"That's not us," Oscar snapped, cutting his mother off.

"Son." Orville's eyes narrowed at Oscar's sharp tone.

Lucy squeezed Orville's hand, stopping his words. "It's

okay," she said, looking at Orville. She turned her eyes back to Oscar. "Hear me out, just for argument's sake."

Oscar nodded, "Sorry, Momma. I didn't mean to be rude."

"When two people love each other, like your father and I, their problems become your problems. You accept them all, the good, the bad, and the ugly." Lucy laid her head on Orville's shoulder, but continued to stare at her son. "Your love for a person won't change who they are, not for long. Only God can do that. That's why I asked where she was with her walk with the Lord. He's the One she needs right now, son. First Him, then, if it's meant to be . . . you."

Chapter Eighteen

Oscar's truck lumbered down the road back toward town. His thoughts flew through his brain at a much faster pace than his vehicle, the cow fields and pine trees easing by through the window unnoticed. He appreciated his parent's concern, he really did. He'd gone to them for help, true, but they were off base with his and Fifer's relationship. Weren't they?

He did have feelings for Fifer, that was certain, but a person didn't fall in love with another person after a few weeks. He simply liked her—a lot, was attracted to her—a lot. Keeping the promise he'd made to give her space while her foot healed had been hard. No, hard was a gross understatement. It had been almost impossible. He'd taken Festus to the backyard when he got home from work in the evenings and found the spot where he could see through the window in her backdoor. He'd toss the ball to his dog in that direction, then search through her curtained window to find her shadow. Looking for any trace of her to balm his need to see how she was doing.

He'd stood with his ear to the wall adjoining his side of the house to hers and listened for sounds, any sounds from her. He'd picked up his phone dozens of times every day to see if she had texted. Who was he kidding? He didn't obsess like this about friends. He didn't stare at his ceiling through the night, reliving scenes in his head of any other friend he'd ever had. No, he had admitted last weekend that he was falling for her. He'd halfway hoped that some time apart would cool those feelings, give him back his rational head. It hadn't.

Oscar cared for Fifer. Maybe his parents were right. It was possible that he even loved her—a little. If he did love her. Even thinking the words in a factual way sent a wave of fear through him. His eyes narrowed. If he did love her, it was time to take the bull by the horns and find out what was going on. He'd stayed away from her all week, even when she'd returned to work after taking a few days off. She'd had plenty of time to get over her injury and whatever that thing was that happened in the emergency room.

He pushed on the gas pedal, speeding up his pace. If he really loved her, and not like a friend, then it was time to talk, to find out how she felt. They needed to talk. They were going to talk, even if he did have to actually break down her front door. She'd get over it. This was too important to let her bully him around.

"What in the world?" A few minutes later, Oscar pulled his truck into its usual spot in front of his side of the duplex and stared at the scene across the way. Festus climbed into his lap, eager to get out of the truck, but Oscar eased him back to his side of the seat. He reached behind the seat and got the dog's leash and snapped it to his collar. "You are going inside, boy. I don't know what's going on over there, but it's no place for you."

He got out of the truck, and as expected, Festus leapt toward Fifer's yard. Oscar wrapped the leash around his wrist and pulled him back. He wrangled Festus into his house, shut the door behind him, then turned to Fifer's front porch. The Miata was parked, if you could call it that, sideways across Fifer's lawn, the driver's side front tire on the bottom step of her porch, the car door open. He walked across the grass, stepped onto her porch, and looked into the car. Her purse was still laying on the passenger's seat.

Oscar shut the car door and turned, stepping over to her front door. "Fifer?" He knocked on the door. No answer. "Fifer?" He turned the doorknob. Unlocked. "I'm coming in." He squinted his eyes, trying to see. Why were the lights off? Oscar wrinkled his nose. What was that odor? The evening sun fell through the front window curtains, and Oscar's eyes adjusted to the sight in front of him. A couple of empty alcohol bottles lay on their sides on her coffee table. Fifer lay on her couch curled in a fetal position; another empty bottle wrapped tightly in her arms.

"Fifer?" Oscar stepped over to the couch and dropped to his knees. "Fifer." He put one hand over his nose and mouth as the scent of stale urine wafted up from the damp cushion. He pulled his other hand back from the cushion. He shoved a mass of tangled curls away from her face and stretched open her eyelid with his fingertips. "Wake up, Fifer." Oscar's heart leaped into his throat. He'd heard of people dying of alcohol poisoning. What was she drinking? He picked up an empty bottle from the coffee table and looked at the label. Vodka. He was not a drinker and didn't know anything about alcohol, but three bottles of Vodka seemed like a lot for someone as thin as she was. "Fifer!" Panic edged his voice. "Wake up!"

"Nooo," Fifer slurred. She hugged the bottle closer. "Let me sleep."

Oscar pulled in a slow breath, and his heart left his throat and went back to its regular spot in his chest. "Fifer. Sit up. It's time to wake up." He eased the bottle from her grasp and set it on the coffee table with the other two. Didn't hung over people need coffee? Seemed like that's what everybody did in the movies. Oscar ran his hand slowly across her cheek, sticky with her saliva. I'm going to fix us some coffee, Fifer. I'll be right back. You . . ." He looked from her closed eyes, her face with drool dripping from the corner of her mouth, to her tangled hair. "You stay right there."

He hurried to her kitchen and looked at the Keurig sitting on her counter. He searched the cabinets and found a couple of mugs, then popped a k-cup of bold black Columbian into the machine and pushed start. How had his parents known she was a drinker? How had he not known? He thought back as he switched out the first mug and started the second. She'd never appeared intoxicated. Not once. She was definitely drunk out of her mind now.

He picked up the smoking mugs and stepped back into the living room. Fifer sat on the couch staring straight ahead with red-streaked eyes, hair hanging in her face. She was sitting up. That was a good sign. "Here." He sat beside her, dodging the smelly, wet spot he'd found earlier, and placed one mug on the coffee table. He lifted her ice-cold hand and wrapped her fingers around the other mug. "Hold this." He watched her raise her other hand to the mug, but didn't let go until he was sure she wouldn't drop the steaming coffee in her lap. She cradled the mug shakily with both hands, not moving any further. He stood, his eyes searching the room. A basket full of fuzzy blankets sat in the corner. He grabbed one from the pile and returned to the couch, tucking the blanket around her legs. "Here," he said again. He placed his hand over her shaking ones and raised the mug to her lips. He watched her take the first sip, then continued to help her drink the coffee, silently waiting for her to awaken enough to talk.

"This is why I can't be around you." Fifer's voice was hoarse.

"Drink a little more."

She took another sip, then pushed the mug away. "You weren't supposed to see my monster." Fifer continued to stare down, her hair covering most of her face. "But." She lifted her chin, her eyes rising to Oscar's face through strands of fiery hair. "Here you are. What do you think, Oscar Robinson? How do you like the real Fifer McKenzie? Pretty, huh."

"I think." Oscar reached down and took the tilting mug from her hands before it spilled into her lap. "You have had a rough few days." He set the half-empty mug on the coffee table beside his untouched one. "Let's get you sober, and then we can talk."

"Why?" Fifer sniffed, and a tear ran down her face. "There's nothing to talk about. You're." She waved her hand up and down in front of him. "You're good. And me? Well, as you can see, I'm messed up." She threw a thick mass of hair out of her face. "Oil and water, you and me. We don't mix, Oscar. I've fallen into my oily pit. I haven't been here in." She paused and wiped the back of her hand across her nose. "Five years—I think. I've kept it under control, been strong for five years. But just a few weeks with you and . . . ." A shuddering breath escaped her chest. "Here I am, my true colors spilling out for all to see."

"It's the cut." Oscar took both of her pale hands in his. "The trip to the emergency room and all the pain from your cut did this, Fifer. It's going to be alright."

"No." Fifer shook her head, blowing her stale breath into Oscar's face. "The cut was nothing." She pulled one hand free from Oscar's grip and reached up. Her fingers ran along his jaw and stopped, her palm cradling the side of his face. "Don't you see? To let you into my fortress, I had to make a crack in my wall. I've been building that wall for a decade. I knew better than to chip out a door. For you." She smiled a small, sad smile. "I let you in, but the monster found my weak spot, like he did before, and he came out. And." She pulled down her hand. Her shoulders shrugged. "Here I am. I'm the monster, Oscar. You can't have one without the other. I'm lying in the slime with the snake around my neck."

Wetness filled Oscar's eyes. "You, Fifer McKenzie, are not a monster. You have a—problem—but you are not a monster. We will get you some help. I know somebody who can get you straightened out."

"You don't understand." Fifer's sad, green eyes connected with Oscar's worried, blue eyes. "I've conquered the monster, the problem, before. I know what to do to be a decent person, but it takes all of me to do it." She swallowed. Her fingers reached up and wiped away a tear from his lashes. "I can't have love in my life and stay sober. I've tried and I always end up like this. The real Fifer McKenzie always escapes."

"This is not the real Fifer McKenzie." Oscar reached his arms around Fifer and pulled her to his chest. "You don't have to do this alone. Not anymore." His hand stroked her head. "I am going to help you."

"Oscar?"

"Yeah?"

"I'm going to be sick." Fifer lifted her head and lurched forward, vomit spewing all over Oscar's lap. A second later, she raised her head. "You don't want this. You say you do today, but believe me, you don't. This mess is not yours. You deserve better."

Oscar forced down the gag rising in his throat. He didn't look down at the disgust in his lap. His eyes searched her face. "Don't push me away, Fifer. Please." His nostrils flared at the acid smell of what was in his lap. Did he really want to commit to this? To her? *I don't have a choice. I love this woman.* "I'm going to be here for you." He looked at her face, full of doubt. "I'll prove that I'm tough enough to handle you. And your monster."

A glimmer of hope sparked in Fifer's eyes. "I can be mean."

"I know."

"Selfish."

"I've already seen it."

"Bossy."

"That's a given."

A small smile formed on Fifer's lips, and she hiccupped. "I just puked in your lap, and you're still here."

"I'm not a wimp. It takes more than a bad hangover to get rid of me."

Fifer's brow creased. "Oscar, this is me. Bad breath, vomit, the whole nine yards. This is what I fight every single day of my life." Her eyes looked down at his hands, then raised slowly back to his face. "Are you sure this is who you want to be your . . ." The words faded away.

"I'm sure, Fifer." Oscar's heart squeezed. "But will you let me get you some help? You—we—can't do this on our own."

"Okay." Fifer's red eyes blinked, and fear crept into her face. "But not from my father."

"No." Oscar frowned. "Not from your father."

Chapter Nineteen

There were so many things Fifer couldn't remember. Memories that held information. Memories that held pain. None of them held joy. Nothing about being plastered out of her skull had ever brought her joy. Alcohol had been a part of her family for so far back. Not that she'd been drinking . . . or fighting to not drink her entire life. Only her entire adult life—and a few of her teen years.

Adrian McKenzie, Fifer's beautiful mother, was often tipsy, as she liked to call it. Not falling down, black out drunk, like the place Fifer's drinking always seemed to lead. "I have just enough to take the edge off," Mother would say. "Today, the edge is rather large."

At fourteen, Fifer had gone to her first boy/girl function, a highly chaperoned school dance. She was a gawky, too tall, red-headed mess, and kids could be cruel. She'd come in from the dance, went to her room, and slammed the door, letting her Irish temper flair. Her mother, drink in hand, made her way to Fifer's side, snuggled up beside her. She listened as Fifer poured her heart out about her horrible red hair, her skinny legs, Jenny Foster dancing with the guy Fifer wanted to dance with, intentionally stealing him away when she could have found someone else.

The details got fuzzy here, but somehow Adrian McKenzie offered her daughter a sip from her glass. "Now don't tell your father." Fifer did remember that part. That was a reoccurring theme with Mother. "Let's not worry your father. He has a little bit of a temper." Or "there's no need to upset your father over this. What he doesn't know won't hurt him. Or me."

Fifer's mother, with her terribly misguided good intentions to help her daughter sleep, had set Fifer's path. The young teen had taken to it like a fish to water. She didn't become a complete sop immediately. To be fair, her mother had not encouraged her to drink alcohol very often. But junior high was rough, and the alcohol was right there in the house. Nobody paid attention when she sneaked a little up to her room from time to time. By the time Fifer was seventeen, she was getting drunk out of her head every weekend.

Her mother threatened to have Fifer put in rehab if she didn't tone it down. Drinking was one thing, but being brought home in the middle of the night falling down drunk four weekends in a row was quite another thing. How in the world did Fifer expect to keep this from her father?

She'd graduated from high school in May with plans to start college in the fall. Father wanted her to get a business degree. "You aren't going to be a weight around my neck like your mother, girl. You will earn your keep or end up in a ditch like that brother of mine." That was fine by Fifer. She didn't have a clue what she wanted to do. Business was as good as the next thing. She just wanted to get out of the house.

Two weeks after graduation, on a Saturday night, she had gone out with friends. Trudy, the friend who didn't drink, had driven Fifer and another girlfriend to a bar. Her friend turned eighteen earlier that week, and Fifer would be eighteen in a couple of months, but her fake ID was a good one. No more getting a friend to buy booze from the liquor store and driving down near the edge of town to get drunk.

Fifer wasn't sure how it happened. Her memory lapses when she was intoxicated had already started, but somehow that night, Trudy and her sober friend left without her. It didn't matter. She'd probably picked a fight with one of them. She was prone to do that, but since she often bought the booze and food on their excursions, she kept getting invited along. What mattered was the bartender called her house to get someone to pick her up.

Her father wasn't home. Was he ever? That left tipsy Mother to come to her rescue. Fifer remembered getting in the car in the pouring rain, her mother's voice not in time with the wipers. "Fifer, this has got to stop," Mother slurred, pulling away from the curb. Fifer had closed her eyes, blocking out the droning of her mother's voice.

The next time she remembered opening her eyes, she was flat on her back, the smell of wet pine needles and fall leaves filling her nostrils. Freezing rain splattered icy cold in her face. Everything hurt everywhere. Lights blared through the dark, and a stranger's voice cut into the pounding in her head. "Get the stretcher over here! This one's alive."

A week later, her brain finally started functioning again. "Where's Mother?" Fifer looked at her father, strolling into her hospital room dressed in one of his expensive black suits. "How long before I can go home?"

"I waited as long as I could, but the doctor said with the swelling on your brain, there was no way to tell when you'd wake up. If ever." Louis McKenzie's explanation was all about the facts. "I buried her today. You can go to the graveside when you get out of here."

"Mother's dead?" Fifer's chest closed up. She tried to pull in air, but couldn't breathe. Screaming filled her ears. Two nurses rushed into the room and held down the arm that wasn't in a cast. The one she was ripping out her hair with. They forced her to be still and put something in her IV. Fifer's eyes darted around the room, and she fought, tried to remember what had happened. She couldn't. She blinked, relaxing as the medication took over. She watched her father, the only parent she had left, turn his back and walk out.

Fifer stayed in the private hospital room for another week, her left arm in a cast, cuts and abrasions from head to foot. No visitors came, Father's orders. "The doctor says you need to be kept calm." She hadn't argued. Arguing with Father never worked in her favor anyway.

The day of her discharge, Father came in at his usual time. "We need to talk about the accident."

"I didn't call Mother to come get me." Fifer's hands shook, and she hid them under the covers. She tried to wrap her head around everything that happened. "I would never have put her in danger that way."

"Someone called her." Louis McKenzie stood by the hospital bed. He never stayed long enough to sit down. "It might as well have been you. You were the reason she came. She's gone now, and that's not going to change, but some other things are."

"I'm not going to drink anymore, Father." Fifer slipped her shaking hands out from under the covers. "You don't have to worry about that."

"You see, Fifer, I do have to worry about that." Father's voice was stern, as usual, daring her to question his authority as she'd often done in the past. "When you drive drunk and kill a person, that doesn't just go away."

"But . . . I wasn't driving." Fifer's voice trembled. "Was I? Mother was."

"Not according to the reports." Louis McKenzie stared at his daughter. "Your body was on the ground on the driver's side. If I hadn't pulled a few strings, you would be looking at manslaughter."

"Jail?"

"Prison, Fifer. You're seventeen, but they could decide to try you as an adult. Be thankful I have a few connections around here, or you would be going before a judge tomorrow. Do as I tell you, and this will all get buried in your juvenile record."

"I." Fifer swallowed. "What's going to happen now?"

"You are going into rehab. You're going to work your behind off there, learn how to get this drinking under control. Then you're going to come to work for me and do exactly what I tell you to do. From now on I'm going to keep a close eye on you."

"What about college?"

"You can take courses along while you're working. I don't trust you enough to do this any other way. You're too much like your mother and some other people in our family. Weak."

"What if?" Fifer licked her upper lip and winced. The swelling was gone, but the scab was dry and tender. Her tongue pulled in and found the gap where her front tooth had once been. It settled there. "What if I don't want to go to rehab?"

"Do it my way, and you can be free with a career in my business." Louis McKenzie shrugged his shoulders. "Or don't. Your way is taking your chance with the judge. You may go to prison, or you may not. You can get a job flipping burgers. That's about all you're good for. Don't think I'm going to continue to pay the bills for you, not after what you've done. Do it my way, or get what you deserve."

Fifer pushed the ancient memories to the background and rolled over in the bed. How had she gotten upstairs? Flashes of the weekend came to mind. Driving back to the liquor store for a few more bottles, falling down as she walked to her car, taking a coffee mug from Oscar's hands. Had he carried her up here? Who else would have? She rolled over and sat on the side of the bed, running her tongue over the sticky goo in her mouth. Her head pounded. She never had headaches except for the ones that came around after the drinking.

She stretched her shoulders and stood, holding onto her bedframe to steady her wobbly legs. Hydration and food. Some people thought pumping yourself with coffee got you straightened out faster. It might work for others, but for her, getting fluids and food into her system was always the quickest way to get back on her feet.

She slogged to the bathroom and climbed into the shower, scrubbing herself from one end to the other. No mercy. She had slipped into the pit, but she would not stay there. Drill sergeant control was needed to get herself back in working order, and she had that. She finished in the bathroom, then threw on some pajama pants and a tee-shirt. What time was it? If she was late for work, she'd blame it on her foot. She sat on the bed and looked at her stitched-up instep. The dressing was gone, but at least she hadn't re-injured the place. The wound was closed, and a thin scab was forming along the line on the cut.

A whiff of bacon and coffee floated through her open bedroom door. A flash of Oscar holding her to his chest filled her mind. What had happened over the weekend? Why would he be in her kitchen? He must have seen her . . . the hidden her. She put on her slippers and headed downstairs. It was a relief, really. At least she didn't have to hide that part of her from him anymore. The fact that he was actually here this morning, or this afternoon, whatever it was, only spoke of what a good person he was.

She walked through the living room, taking in the pillow and blanket on the couch. Had Oscar slept in her living room? Other than that, everything looked in order. Her nares flared at the smell of Pine Sol coming from the couch. What had happened over there? Heat rushed to her cheeks. Oscar must have cleaned up her mess. She was a neat freak sober, but that sort of flipped when she fell off the wagon.

Fifer stepped silently into the kitchen and leaned against the island bar. Oscar stood at the stove, his back to her. His broad shoulders filled out his tee-shirt, his black hair barely skimming its collar. "Good morning."

Oscar turned around, egg turner in hand. "Good morning. How do you like your eggs?"

"Fried, but scrambled is fine, too." Fifer stepped to the coffeemaker and started brewing herself a cup. "What time is it?"

"About six-thirty." Oscar lifted several pieces of bacon from the skillet, then opened the egg carton beside the stove. "How are you feeling?"

"I have a headache, but it will pass." Fifer picked up her coffee mug and sipped. "I was afraid I'd overslept. I can finish that up so you can go home and get ready for work."

"I talked to Bill and Grant yesterday." Oscar tilted the skillet and sloshed the hot bacon grease over the egg with the turner. "They know we won't be in today either."

"Either?" Fifer pulled in a deep breath and rolled her eyes. "How long was I out? What day is it?"

"It's Tuesday."

"Good grief. I really tied one on."

"Yeah. Seems so." Oscar put the egg on a plate with a couple of pieces of bacon and handed it to Fifer. "After we eat, I'll drive us out to Eric's place. He's looking forward to meeting you."

Eric? Who was Eric? She took the plate from Oscar's hand. She could pretend to remember everything, but why? He'd already seen her at her worst. Might as well get everything straightened out in her head so she could figure out what she'd agreed to. "There's something you should know about me."

"Yeah?" Oscar's back was to her again. He cracked three eggs into the skillet and stirred them with the turner. "What's that?"

"When I get—like I was this weekend—I can't remember much. I had an accident several years ago and got a concussion. Things would be fuzzy before that happened, but since then I." She paused, watching Oscar turn to face her. "I don't have a clue who Eric is or why we are meeting him."

"Eric is a family friend." Oscar turned off the stove burner and stepped over to Fifer. His hand reached out and smoothed an out-of-control curl on the side of her head. "He knows what you are going through and can help."

"Eric, huh?"

"Yes, Eric. You said you would let me help you."

"How bad was I?"

"I don't have anything to compare this weekend to, but you did throw up in my lap, and I'm pretty sure you peed on your couch."

Fifer's eyes stretched wide. "I guess I owe you one, huh?"

"Come with me to meet Eric, and we'll call it even."

"I have a feeling meeting this Eric won't make up for everything I put you through, but I'll go." Fifer looked down at her plate, then back up at Oscar. "Don't get your hopes up, Oscar. I'm an alcoholic. I keep it controlled by keeping everyone away. That's what works."

"Just give my way a chance, Fifer. Give me a chance."

Chapter Twenty

Eric Weathers, Oscar's family friend, did not look like what Fifer had expected. Oscar pulled his truck into a parking lot on the old side of town, not too far from their office. "What are we doing here?" She looked around. "I thought we were meeting your friend."

"We are." Oscar nodded to a closed-up food truck several yards away. "He doesn't open for the lunch crowd until eleven, but he's already in there, or nearby." Oscar opened his truck door. "Come on. I should have already brought you to have lunch here, anyway. Eric is the sausage dog king of Alabama." He grinned at Fifer. "Maybe even the world."

Fifer looked through the windshield at the dingy, white trailer attached to a dually truck. There was no advertising on the side of the trailer, and the service window on the side had a metal door hinged at the top, closing the place up tight. She looked as Oscar shut his truck door and started across the lot. Might as well get this over with.

She stepped out of the truck, watching carefully where she placed her foot. She was scheduled to go to the doctor later this week for a follow up and hopefully get the stitches out. It was so much better, but she was still careful how she placed her foot on the ground. Especially in an abandoned parking lot with grass and weeds growing through the cracks and loose gravel scattered along to slip her up.

A tall burly man stepped around the edge of the truck and wrapped Oscar in a bearhug, making Oscar look like a gangly kid. Fifer smiled. Oscar did not seem to be the lovey-dovey type. She'd seen him around his sister, his father, and one of his brothers. She couldn't remember which brother, but he worked at the Blue Hotel. None of the family had hugged Oscar like this man had.

"Fifer, this is Eric Weathers," Oscar said when she reached their side. "He is a family friend. I've known him my entire life."

"Nice to meet you, Fifer." Eric wiped his beefy paw on a white canvas apron tied across his middle, then shook her hand. "Y'all come around back here and have a seat. Let me grab us a bottle of water."

Fifer watched the bald lumberjack of a man disappear around the food truck. She looked at Oscar and raised her eyebrows.

"Trust me." Oscar grinned.

"Lead on." Fifer waved her hand in front of her. Her phone buzzed, and she pulled it from the pocket of her yoga pants. Her father's face appeared on the screen. "I'll be right there." She looked at Oscar's worried expression and forced a smile. "Give me just a second." Oscar disappeared around the food truck and Fifer answered the call. "Hello, Father."

"I've been trying to reach you since Friday."

"I've been under the weather." Fifer turned and looked out toward the brick buildings and sidewalks of Red Creek, opening for their daily business. She breathed in a lungful of the early morning air. "What do you want?"

"Do I need to send Joseph down?"

"No." Fifer kept her voice calm but firm. Joseph was her father's "right hand, no questions asked, follow orders, and get results" man. The man had been to their house when she was a kid and through her teen years. He didn't have an official office at her father's business, but he was always around. He was quiet, always in the background, and kept a permanent scowl on his face. He reminded her of a bulldog, a hungry bulldog. When she was finished here in Red Creek getting the dinner theater up and running, hiring a few of the locals for lower positions, Joseph would come in and run the place while he found the right sort of people to truly take over the business and do the backhanded dealings her father had planned. "I had a stomach thing. It didn't slow down the work. Everything is still on schedule."

"You cut your foot, then a stomach thing. Don't try to jerk me around, Fifer. The next time I call, you had better answer on the first ring. Don't forget who pays your salary. Don't forget who knows things."

Fifer looked at her phone, the screen blank where her father hung up in her ear. She pulled her shoulders back and took in the small, peaceful town in front of her. A burning formed in her gut. It would be so, so easy to throw in the towel. To get in her car, leave Red Creek, leave her father, disappear from everything and everyone. Would anybody really care about her being gone?

"Fifer?"

Fifer turned to Oscar, standing at the edge of the food truck a few feet away. He stuck out his hand, offering her a sweaty bottle of water. He would care. She pushed back a tear and took the water. She was just emotional from the weekend, the alcohol leaving her system. It always made her forget her mess of a life, but the price of forgetting was the rollercoaster of regret and other emotions that came along afterwards. It had been a few years since she'd gone through it, but it was back this morning, same ole, same ole cycle. "Thanks." She smiled, putting on a steady, normal face. The aroma of frying pork filled her senses as she stepped around the food truck behind Oscar. "Smells interesting around here."

A few minutes later, Fifer watched Oscar walk to his vehicle and drive away, leaving her and Eric to talk. They migrated to Eric's truck for privacy.

"I know I'm an alcoholic, Eric." Fifer smiled at the bald man with tattoos running up and down his biceps, disappearing under his tee-shirt and reappearing on his neck. "I've been through the program . . . more than once. It helped me figure out a way to control the drinking."

"Yet, here you are."

Fifer looked out the windshield. "I thought I had it figured out. And I have got it figured out if I keep doing things the way I've been doing them." She watched a young woman with a baby bump get out of her car parked on the street nearby. The woman leaned over and kissed the man, who walked around the vehicle to meet her. "But." Fifer's voice cracked. "I'm not sure I can continue on . . . being who I am." She turned to Eric. "I've hurt so many people, you know?"

"I know." Eric opened the console between them and handed her a paper napkin. He waited while she wiped her nose. "Fifer, you've been through the program, but you still think you can control the drinking. Just because you can say you're an alcoholic doesn't mean you are in recovery." Fifer swallowed and nodded, but didn't say anything. "You have to admit—to yourself—that you can't control this. You have to be willing to give yourself to God. He's the only one who can get you through this."

"In ten years, this is my second time to fall." Fifer folded the napkin and dabbed her eyes. "And if I hadn't met Oscar."

"Do you really think Oscar's the problem?"

"No." A sob escaped Fifer's throat. "He's wonderful. But I let my guard down and now." She wiped her nose again. "Now I'm a mess and I can't fix it. If I shut him out, I might be able to stay sober, but I'm not sure I can live like that. Not anymore. It's too hard, and I've hurt so many people. I've tried to be good, find something good inside of me to hang onto, but it's just not there."

"The Bible says no one is good except God alone. If you want peace, real peace, Fifer, you have got to give it all to God." Eric tilted his head forward and looked into her face. "I think deep in your heart you already know that."

"You don't know how bad I am. What I have done."

"God knows. He's known all along. You aren't hiding anything from Him. You just have to surrender to Him. If you will give Him your life, messed up as it is, He will carry you. You can lean on Him until you are where you can walk again. But even then, you have to let God direct your steps. The good you are looking for doesn't come from inside of you. It only comes from God."

"Is that what you did? Give God your mess?"

"Yes." Eric smiled. "A long time ago I was like you, except probably worse. If God hadn't used a nosy friend to get into my business and help me see the truth, I would be dead and in hell right now."

Fifer flipped down the visor and looked at herself in the mirror. If she continued on the path she was going, rebuilt her armor, pushed Oscar away, tried to do things on her own, she might last a little while, but did she really want to be that person? Always be at war with herself, always hiding her true feelings behind a rock-hard façade just so she could survive? She'd harmed so many people, had so many secrets. *God, I can't live like this anymore. Please help me see what I need to do.*

Tears poured from Fifer's eyes, and she turned to Eric. "I'm not sure about the rest yet, but I know I can't keep being the way I am. I need a sponsor. "

"I can do that." Eric took her hand. "We have meetings at the church several nights a week. I'll give you my number if you need me in between."

"What now?"

"Let's start by letting me pray with you. God has a plan for your life, Fifer, just like he had a plan for me. You've made the first step. He'll guide you if you surrender."

Fifer sniffed and nodded. "Surrender isn't easy for me."

"You surrendered to that bottle." Eric smiled. "Why not try surrendering to the One who loves you so much that he died for you?"

Fifer bowed her head. Eric's words flowed through her as she listened to his prayer. He prayed for God to do whatever it would take to make Fifer see Him, the creator of the universe. Whatever it took for her to come to Him and give Him her will so that He could bless her with His love. She swallowed the lump rising in her throat. *God help me.*

A couple of hours after Oscar drove away, his phone buzzed with a text from Fifer. He set down his coffee.

Can you come pick me up?

I'll be right there.

He stood from his desk and tossed his Styrofoam cup in the trash. Bill had raised an eyebrow when he saw Oscar slip into his office in his cargo shorts, tee-shirt, and tennis shoes, but he hadn't said anything. It wasn't like Oscar was going to see anyone work related today. Technically, he wasn't even there. He looked around his office and sighed. He'd been working at this job for ten years. Five years longer than he'd planned. He walked out of the office and closed the door. Now was not the time to worry about his own life. Fifer needed him. He'd promised to be there for her, and he would not break his word.

He loved the woman. He hadn't planned on it, had denied it, but there it was. He'd only known her a short time, but his feelings for her had slammed him, tackled him, refused to let him go. Now that he admitted he loved her, he would do everything in his power to help her overcome this addiction. He didn't know the story of how it had happened, but it didn't matter. Like his mother said, her problem had become his problem. Her monster, as she'd called it the other night when she was drunk out of her mind, was another name for addiction. This was not how he saw his life going. Not at all, but for once he didn't care.

He got in the truck and drove the short distance to the lot where Eric had parked his food truck for months, drawing a nice lunch time crowd. "Lord, I know you have a plan in all of this. I love this woman. Please work it out. She needs You. I need her. I don't know how this all fits together with my plan, the plan I thought You gave me, but I give it all to You. Please work this out, God. I want to somehow make a life with Fifer, but if that is not in Your plan, help me accept Your will, but please, Lord, save Fifer. Take her addiction away and fill her with You."

Chapter Twenty-
One

Oscar pulled into the parking lot and looked across at the food truck, the window now open for the early lunch crowd. Jimmy, Eric's current sausage slinger, stood in the window beside Fifer. Oscar laughed. Fifer had crammed her beautiful red curls into a spidery hair net, and she was handing sausage dogs wrapped in their silver wrappers out the window to the customers. She was taking their money like she'd been working with Eric for years.

Oscar stepped into line behind the guy who cut his hair and looked at the other people from around town. The few men and women in business attire mixed in with the farmers, road workers, housewives, and a few teens who had probably checked out of school to come eat lunch.

Fifer turned from where she was getting more of the pork links wrapped in the soft bread from the steamer behind her. "Hey, you," she said, grinning at Oscar as she passed the food wrapped in silver foil to the barber. "Can I interest you in a sausage dog for the road?"

"I usually order three. Put however many you want for

yourself in with mine, too." Oscar pulled his wallet from his back pocket. He put the money in Fifer's hand and looked around while she bagged up their lunch. People were chatting, eating, or carrying their food to their vehicles to eat on the way back to work. He smiled at a lady at the edge of the window as he waited. She squirted an ample amount of mustard on her sausage, then wrapped it back up.

Eric turned from the other end of the little trailer where he was manning the griddle. "Oscar. Man, am I glad to see you. This woman has been bossing me around for two hours." He grinned at Fifer as she rolled her eyes. "See if you can persuade her to leave so I can have my boss position back."

Eric wrapped his enormous biceps around Fifer's narrow shoulders, and a twinge of jealousy floated up from somewhere inside of Oscar. Yes, he was definitely in love with this woman. "I take it you two are getting along well?"

"Like two messed up peas in a sausage smelling pod, my friend," Eric said, chuckling as Fifer elbowed him in the gut. Oscar looked down at Fifer. "I'll see you at the meeting?"

"I'll be there," Fifer said, her smile turning from playful to sincere. "And thank you."

"I'm only doing what someone else did for me." Eric squeezed her shoulders, then looked at Oscar. "Tell Orville Robinson just because he's living in a fancy new house and married to a famous singer doesn't mean he's too good to stop by and tell his friend hello every once in a while." Eric took his arm from around Fifer's shoulder. "I haven't seen him except at church in over a month."

"Part of that is my fault." Fifer untied the white apron from around her middle, then picked up the plastic bag containing their food. "He's cleaning out the movie theater. It was crammed full of stuff. I imagine it's the busiest he's been in quite a while."

"That's no excuse." Eric took the apron from Fifer's hand. "Tell him I'm supposed to be higher up on his list than his junk."

Fifer disappeared behind them through the little door on the trailer, the food bag in her hand. Eric looked down at Oscar. "I'm praying for her and for you. God's working on her, so don't you give up the fight."

"I won't." Oscar reached up through the window and shook the older man's hand. "I can promise you that."

Fifer stepped around the side of the food truck as Oscar turned away from the window. "You ready?"

"If you are." Oscar reached over and touched the black, spidery web of the hair net clinging to Fifer's forehead. "Hey. Let me take a picture. I have a feeling this look might be a new one for you."

Fifer reached up and pulled the net from her hair before Oscar could retrieve his phone. "Don't you dare." Red curls cascaded onto her shoulders, and she shook out her mane. "There're some looks I'd rather not keep for posterity."

They weaved through the vehicles in the beat-up parking lot back to Oscar's truck parked at the curb. Fifer climbed into the cab and waited while Oscar retrieved a couple of sports drinks from his cooler in the back. He slid in behind the steering wheel a couple of seconds later and handed her a sweaty bottle of blue Gatorade. "Well?" Fifer asked. She watched him start the truck and waited for him to ask about the last two hours. Oscar unscrewed the Gatorade top without saying a word.

"Well," Oscar finally said, setting his drink in the holder. He reached to the dash and adjusted the air conditioner. "How are you doing?" His brow wrinkled. "Unless you need a bit of time to process everything and don't want to talk about it. I'm sort of new with this kind of thing and don't know what I'm supposed to do or say."

"This knight in shining armor thing?" Fifer set her drink beside his, then laid her hand on his muscular upper arm. "You seem to be a natural for the part." She ran her tongue over her dry lips and pulled in a deep breath. "I'm starting AA with Eric on Thursday."

"That's good." Oscar turned his shoulders in the truck seat to face Fifer. "I'm not sure exactly what happened with Eric in the past, but it was before I was born. A woman died that he was dating, and he served a little time for his involvement in whatever happened to her. He was Dad's friend before all that, and when he came back to Red Creek after serving his time, I was a kid. Him and Dad started hanging out together, then Eric started working for Dad at the junk store. He went to church with us and was at the house a lot, too. According to Dad, he's the one that got our church to start the AA program."

"I appreciate you bringing me to him." Fifer looked down at the plastic bag between them. She pulled out two sausage dogs and passed one to Oscar. She stared down at the foil wrapper in her hands, fiddling with the paper. "I have this dream where I'm covered in slime and mud. There's this enormous snake wrapped around me, and it's dragging me deeper and deeper into the mess." Fifer pinched the silver paper and rubbed it between her fingers. "You and everyone around me are watching me. And I'm there too, in my work clothes, staring down at the me on the ground." She looked up at Oscar and laughed self-consciously. "We're all watching, staring at the me on the ground struggling against the mud and the snake, and nobody can do anything to help me."

"That's . . ."

"Crazy. I know." Fifer blinked back tears. "You are there looking at me, sort of like you are now, but you can't help me."

"Fifer." Oscar put down his lunch and reached across the truck. He took Fifer's hands in his. "I wasn't going to say crazy. I was going to say that it's sort of the truth."

"The truth?" Fifer frowned. "I've tried to figure the dream out, and I think the snake is my drinking. I think it's killing me or something, and nobody has the power to stop it. At least that's what I thought." Fifer looked through the windshield toward the food truck. "But after this morning, and you bringing me to Eric, I figured it was just a crazy dream."

"I think the snake could be the alcohol—for you." Oscar said the words slowly. "It's different for different people. We all have, or had, a snake in our lives at one time or another."

"What do you mean?" Fifer looked at Oscar.

"I think the snake is the sin that controls us all. The devil knows we all have at least one weakness, and he uses that to entice us to sin. For some people the sin is obvious." Oscar raised his palm. "Like the alcohol with you and Eric. For other people it's harder to see. But we all have a sin problem, Fifer. And no matter what you read or what people tell you, nobody can get you free from your sin but Jesus. Just like in your dream, we see you struggling, but we can't rescue you. We are all helpless without Him."

"I know the Bible story." Fifer turned her gaze back to the window. "I had to memorize the plan of salvation for one of the rehab programs I was in. But." She paused and looked back at Oscar. "I've always thought I was too strong to surrender. That I didn't have it in me. Until today."

"Yeah?" Oscar stared at Fifer's face, his expression not revealing anything. "What happened today?"

"It was something Eric said. I told him what I just told you about not surrendering, and he said I've already surrendered to the alcohol."

"I suppose that's true," Oscar said.

"And if that's the case, then even when I'm not drinking, the alcohol is still controlling me. It keeps me from being honest. It keeps me from caring about others. It has turned me into someone I don't like at all."

"The Bible says we can't have two masters." Oscar's eyes narrowed, remembering things he'd learned over the years from his father. "We have to choose who we are going to serve, but everybody serves something or someone."

"And by not making a conscious choice." Fifer's eyes stretched wide as the meaning dawned on her. "I am automatically choosing to let my sin control me. I'm letting my sin be my master." She stared at Oscar, her mind suddenly opening up to what the verses she'd learned all those years ago meant. "I've sinned, and until I give my sinful life to Christ, I will always be a slave to my sin."

"That's right." Oscar smiled softly at Fifer. "But when you give your life to Christ, He pays the penalty for your sin with the sacrifice of His sinless life. Then He moves into your life."

"I think that's the problem I've had." Fifer's mouth pressed into a tight line as she searched for the words to explain her feelings. "Even though I didn't realize it until now."

"What? I don't understand."

"Knowing that God—the Father—would be in my life. Controlling it." Fifer blinked several times as she looked at

Oscar, trying to keep the tears at bay. "I've always had a father in my life controlling me. It has not been a good thing."

"But." Oscar lifted his hand and cupped Fifer's cheek. "God is nothing like Louis McKenzie. He loves you, Fifer. He loves you more than I do or am even capable of, and He wants to take care of you. He wants to protect you from sin and from the earthly father that's doing you harm."

Tears rolled down Fifer's cheeks. "I'm ready for a new father." She wiped her eyes and took a deep breath. "I'm ready to give my life, as messed up as it is, to Christ."

Oscar took both of Fifer's hands in his. "I've never done this with anybody before. I mean, I've prayed with people. A lot. Usually my dad, but I've always been the one getting the guidance." He looked Fifer in the eye. "You want to go see my dad? He's fantastic with this kind of thing."

"No, Oscar." Fifer held Oscar's gaze and smiled. "Pray with me. Just hold my hands. I think I know what I need to say." Oscar nodded and bowed his head. Fifer bowed hers, and for a few seconds said nothing. Finally, over the pounding of her heart, the words came. "Dear God, I don't want to be in control. I guess I'm not in control, even though I thought I was." She laughed softly. "What I'm trying to say and making a mess of, is that I want to give you my life. It's not much, and I don't have a clue how to make it better, but I am giving it to you. Please forgive me. For the drinking. For the pain I've caused the people I love, for the pain I've caused other people because of my cowardice. Forgive me for all the things that I've done. You know the list is so long. And ugly." She was silent again for several seconds then whispered, "amen."

Oscar smiled as they lifted their heads. "That was great, Fifer."

"I just spoke from my heart." She smiled back. "It felt good. Honest."

Oscar leaned over and kissed Fifer's damp cheek. "I'm proud of you."

Fifer's heart swelled. "I don't think I would have made it here without you." She smiled at Oscar. "You've seen me at my worst, and yet you're still here."

"Don't worry. I'm not going anywhere. I think you're stuck with me."

"Good. I like it."

Chapter Twenty-Two

It had been a crazy-busy month, with so many things changing, it made Fifer's head whirl. Not so much on the outside, although there was a lot, but things were so different on the inside. For as long as she could remember, she'd been pushing her shoulder against the world, shoving back as hard as she could against everything it threw at her. The weight had been suffocating at times, but she hadn't truthfully known the extent of it until it was gone. Turning her sinful, messed up life over to Christ, knowing she was not alone in her daily grind, knowing God was carrying her enormous burden with the tip of His almighty finger, had changed everything.

The first AA meeting, walking through the door of the church the first time after what she would forever call sausage-dog Tuesday, had been the hardest. Oscar had driven her there. She wouldn't let him come in. She needed to do this part herself. Eric had met her at the door. "The first time is hard, but you got this," he said, no longer in a stained canvas apron or smelling like fried pork. She was surprised by a couple of people in the room. One was the nurse who had helped her that night in the emergency room. Another was Bob, the old man that ran the coffee shop.

She'd talked to the preacher of Oscar's church the following Sunday. Her father did not attend her baptismal service, of course. She hadn't told him about anything. He would see all of this as detrimental to her reputation, and therefore to his reputation as well. He would also see it all as an enormous sign of weakness.

She would have loved to tell her grandmother, her father's mother, about the change in her life, but she couldn't risk the sweet old lady sharing the information with her son. Her grandmother, like many people around her father, had no idea how he truly was. He was such a charming, warm man to the world, especially to his mother. If there was ever a human chameleon, it was Louis McKenzie.

She would tell her grandmother about everything one day, but not until she got a few things figured out. Like how to get out from under her father's thumb. She'd always followed his instructions. Get in, set up the business, get out. Having his daughter come in and get the family business rolling had an air of respectability to it that Louis McKenzie relied on.

Fifer had been meticulously careful to ignore what he did after she turned everything over to Joseph, his right-hand man. Not knowing her father's plans had been easier and safer until now. Turning a blind eye to what she helped her father do was sinful. She'd challenged her father a few times in the past, trying to find out the details about the night her mother died. Her father had spies everywhere and always found out. He enjoyed making her pay for her curiosity, usually by taking it out on anyone or anything Fifer cared for. She had learned to care less and less over the years as a matter of self-preservation. All of that had changed now. She had to face him, but first she had to figure out a way to do this and protect the people of Red Creek.

"Fifer? Is everything okay?"

Fifer turned and smiled at Oscar as they pulled up in front of his father's house. "I'm a little nervous, I guess."

"Why." Oscar killed the truck engine and reached over and squeezed her hand. "You came to lunch the Sunday after you got baptized and met everyone but Ori then. They all love you." He flashed a heart-tugging smile. "Possibly even more than they love me."

"But that was before we were dating, or at least officially dating. And tonight, it's just your parents." Festus stuck his head over the backseat. His long sandpaper tongue licked Fifer's cheek, and she laughed. "I know they're okay with me being your friend, but your girlfriend is different. They know I go to AA, I'm sure." Her eyes dropped down at his hand on top of hers. "I'm sort of damaged goods. That might not sit well with them."

Oscar reached his hand under her chin and lifted her face. "It's going to be fine. I promise."

They got out of the truck, and Festus darted ahead of them and disappeared around the house. The last time they were here, that Sunday after church, Oscar had showed her where the old house place had been that burned down last year. The new house his parents built was further back, butting up to the woods and the path that led down to Red Creek.

They stepped onto the porch, and the sound of a guitar and singing from somewhere inside filled her ears. "They were singing the other time I was here." Fifer stopped at the front door, listening to the song she'd heard occasionally on the radio as a child.

"They're always singing." Oscar opened the screen door. "You'll get used to it. Since they've gotten back together, it seems like that's all they do."

Oscar opened the wooden door without knocking, and

Fifer followed him into the living room. The smell of something enticing and comforting filled their noses. "Anybody home?" Oscar called.

"In the kitchen," Orville answered, the music stopping abruptly. He appeared in the doorway over to the side, Lucy beside him. "I hope you're hungry. With all the practice she's getting, Lucy's becoming a decent cook." He grinned and looked down at his wife. "Oof." Her elbow jabbed into his gut. "Maybe a little better than decent."

"Have we got a few minutes before we sit down to eat?" Oscar looked from his father to his mother. "I need to talk to Dad about something."

Fifer's eyes narrowed. What was on his mind? He hadn't acted like anything was wrong today, or all week, for that matter. It could be something family related or with his father's business. Oscar did keep his father's books for his store. She pushed her lips into a smile. No need to worry. Not yet, anyway.

"I believe so," Lucy Robinson said. "The cornbread has a few more minutes in the oven. Why don't you and Orville step outside for a minute? We will be fine." She looked at Fifer and smiled a reassuring smile. "I'm sure we'll find something to chat about."

Fifer watched Oscar and Orville disappear through the front door, the screen bumping shut behind them. Oscar really did look like a carbon copy of his father, except that Orville's shoulders weren't quite as broad as his son's, and, of course, Orville's hair had grey mixed in with the black. She turned to Lucy, who had stepped up to her side. "I wonder what that's about?"

"Your guess is as good as mine. Probably related to one of Orville's wheeler-dealer junk deals." Lucy chuckled. "Oscar looks more like his daddy than the rest of the kids, no doubt, but he didn't get his father's reckless streak or his joking sense of humor." Lucy led Fifer over to a set of photos on the wall. "I wasn't around when the kids were growing up. They say Orville was a grouch back then." She pointed to a younger version of Oscar in a graduation cap and gown, Orville standing beside him, both men with a scowl on their faces. "It would appear so, but I can't imagine it. Now Oscar, from what I've seen since I've been back, he's strictly a business-man." She turned and looked Fifer in the eye. "Is that what you see?"

"Not . . . exactly." Fifer held Lucy's gaze for a couple of seconds, then looked away. "Which one is this?" She pointed to another photo of a teen propped against the side of an ancient pickup truck.

"That's Ori. Let's see." Lucy looked at the collage of frames. "When the old place burned, Orville lost all the family photos. Of course, I didn't have any, except a few, from when the kids were very young. Thank goodness Sadie, Orville's older sister, had these. She let me make copies. That's Owen." She pointed to a picture of a young man who looked a lot like Oscar, also in a cap and gown, but had an infectious grin on his face. "He and Ori." Her finger moved to the correct person's photo as she spoke. "They have more of Orville's joking side of his personality. Odi." She moved to another photo. "He's serious like Oscar. I guess that comes in handy being a lawyer."

"What about the twins?" Fifer pointed to the young man and woman in their teens standing side by side in what Lucy described as their church clothes.

"Oliver." Lucy's voice softened. "How Orville and I made such a sweet, kind-hearted soul is sort of a mystery. Don't get me wrong. The other boys are wonderful and caring as well, but Oliver is a loving soul."

"What about Olivia?"

"Bless that girl's heart. She inherited my temper and my

hard head." Lucy turned, her eyes twinkling. "Of course, that could have come from Orville too, but he says I have a special type of bullheaded stubbornness that men don't seem to have."

Fifer laughed and looked around the room. "Is that what I think it is?" Her eyes landed on the object across the room, sitting on the mantle over the fireplace.

"Probably." Lucy led Fifer to the Grammy award. "Orville won it years ago for one of his songs. Another man accepted it for him, but never gave it to him. I finally got it back from the guy a few weeks ago." She picked up the edge of the base and pulled out the dollar store receipt dangling from under it. "Not that it matters to Orville. He had it sitting on the refrigerator behind his Stetson."

Fifer's finger ran along the gold rim of the old-timey record player on the statue. She turned slowly to Lucy, who was watching her. "Does it bother you that Oscar and I are dating?"

"How do you mean?"

"I'm sure you've heard that I'm going to the AA meetings at your church." Fifer rolled her lips in and bit down for half a second. "Do you mind Oscar dating a woman who is a recovering alcoholic?"

"Honey." Lucy laid a hand on Fifer's arm. "We all have things in us that are not pretty. Some of them are more visible to the outside world, but believe me, we all have our issues. Now if you hadn't given your life to the Lord before y'all started getting serious, then yeah, I would have said something." A beeper went off in the kitchen. Lucy raised her hand and patted Fifer's cheek. "But the Lord worked all that out in His perfect timing. Only the Lord can truly fix what needs straightening in all of us. Whatever means He uses to do it is between Him and that believer. AA is a tool God is using to help his child." She turned toward the kitchen and motioned for Fifer to follow. "Besides, out of all the Robinson boys, I think Oscar is the one who could deal with that sort of situation the best. It takes a whole lot to ruffle that man's feathers. That's one thing he does get after his father."

Lucy slipped on an enormous pair of red checked oven mitts and opened the oven door. The aroma of fresh baked cornbread mixed with fried chicken and squash casserole made Fifer's stomach growl. "Why don't you step out to the porch and tell the men dinner's ready while I flip this bread," Lucy said, hoisting the iron skillet onto the stovetop.

Fifer stepped onto the porch, her eyes scanning the area. Festus bounded up the steps from the left side of the yard. Fifer turned in that direction. Oscar and Orville stood over by the barbed wire fence separating the yard from the neighboring cow field. Their heads were bowed together like they were praying. Fifer watched silently, awed by the relationship these two men shared. They soon lifted their heads in unison, and Orville hugged his son. *What is that all about?* "Dinner's ready," she called.

Oscar trotted across the yard, followed by his father, walking at a slow, steady gait. Oscar hopped onto the porch and planted a kiss on Fifer's lips.

"What's that for?" Fifer laughed.

"No reason, except that I love you, Fifer McKenzie."

"I love you too, Oscar Robinson," Fifer whispered. They'd never said the words before, and she was a little surprised that this was the time Oscar chose to declare his feelings. It didn't matter, though. Warmth filled her insides. He draped his arm around her shoulder, and they walked into the house together. Whatever he and his father were discussing didn't matter. Nothing else mattered at that moment. They loved each other.

Chapter Twenty-Three

Fifer snuggled next to Oscar and laid her head on his shoulder. "I don't know why everyone picks at your mother about her cooking. Everything was wonderful."

"My family picks about everything." Oscar moved his arm from the steering wheel and took Fifer's hand. "I think that's just something easy to ruffle her feathers with. Plus, she has been hanging out in Olivia's kitchen with her and Aunt Sadie a lot. Maybe she's gotten a few pointers."

Fifer yawned. "If you say so." She lifted her head and looked through the truck lights as Oscar slowed the vehicle and turned down the gravel road leading to his land on Red Creek. "I thought we agreed. No hanky-panky. If we stay in your tent tonight in your sleeping bag, that's going to be a hard rule to follow."

"We're not going to stay all night." Oscar chuckled. "I know you couldn't resist me that long. We haven't been here since the night you cut your foot. I thought it was time to come back for a little visit." The truck hit a particularly large hole in the gravel road, bouncing them both. "I need to go to the gravel pit tomorrow and get a load for this road. Technically, it's just Aunt Sadie's driveway, so I try to keep the holes filled in myself."

"Do you miss not spending your weekends here like you used to?"

"I still come on most weekends." Oscar slowed and turned the truck down the even smaller dirt road leading to his land. "I just do it at times when I know it won't interfere with our time together. Last Saturday and Sunday, I got here at five in the morning and stayed until about nine." Oscar pulled the truck to its usual spot and opened his door. The lights shone across the way into the nearby woods. Festus hopped across the backseat and climbed over Fifer to get out.

"Somebody's happy to be here." Fifer watched the dog disappear into the woods.

Oscar turned off the truck lights and turned on a flashlight. He reached behind the seat and grabbed a second light and a blanket. "I've gone over the ground with a fine-tooth comb. I picked up a few more pieces of glass, but nothing as big as the one you cut your foot on." He handed her the light. "Watch your step anyway."

Fifer slid out of the driver's seat and followed Oscar around the truck to the tailgate, waiting while he let it down and spread out the blanket. The moon was full tonight, lighting up the land like they were under a streetlamp. She flipped off her flashlight and watched Oscar climb into the truck bed. He stepped over to the ever-present ice chest and pulled out two bottles of what he referred to as store-bought tea. The sound of Red Creek flowing gently over the rocks, the crickets, an occasional lowing of a cow in the fields nearby, that's all she heard. A few fireflies danced through the scattered trees that led into the woods off of the creek bank. The peace of being in this place flowed through her. Even the smell of the ice-cold water running over the mossy rocks, the soft scent of earth covered in leaves, all lent to the comfort and feeling of purity this place possessed.

Oscar reached his hand down from where he stood over Fifer in the truck bed. "I thought we could do a little stargazing before we call it a night."

Fifer took his hand, and he helped her climb up beside him. They settled side by side on the blanket and leaned their heads and shoulders against the cool side of the truck. She could imagine them building a little house back here one day and raising a family, such a different view of the future she had envisioned for herself before this man came into her life. Before God came into her life. "Oscar, I want to ask you something."

"Okay." Oscar cracked the seal of the plastic cap of one of the tea bottles and passed it to her. "There is something I want to ask you too. But you go first."

"Alright." Fifer took a sip of the sweet tea and put it between her knees stretched out in front of her. She breathed in the feel of the place and looked up at the sky full of stars. "I've been watching you since I arrived at Red Creek."

"I've been watching you too." Oscar's voice was playful. "Still am. It's turned into my new favorite pastime."

"Well." She scooted away slightly and turned to face him through the dim light. "You come here literally every chance you get. When you're not here, you're out helping your dad fix fence or doing something outside with a neighbor or friend. Even when you're home, you stay in your backyard. You even told me that while you were in college, you took jobs working outside on purpose."

"Yeah?"

"Then why in the world are you an accountant?" Fifer threw long strands of red curls over her shoulder and waited for his answer. She'd been wearing it down a lot more lately.

Oscar's eyes narrowed, and he took a long drink of his tea.

He lowered the plastic bottle and looked up at the sky. His head eventually turned down, and he looked at Fifer's face. "Security. Stability. Knowing I would have a job to help pay the bills if the rest of the family needed me to. That's the short answer."

"Your parents seem to be comfortable. I mean." Fifer smiled, and her white teeth sparkled in the moonlight. "Your father has a Grammy on his mantle he uses for a paperweight."

"Things are a lot different now than they were before Momma came home. Dad is a lot different. He used to be closed up, and now that I look back on it, sort of miserable looking." Oscar shifted his shoulders against the hard metal behind him. "We lived in the family home that was over one hundred years old. It was literally falling down around our ears. Dad relied on a junk business to pay the bills. Us kids thought our family had one foot in the poorhouse for most of our lives. When you live like that, stability means a great deal to you." He reached over and brushed a curl from her face. "But I have a plan, Fifer McKenzie. And it doesn't involve a tie, or a suit."

"Tell me."

Oscar turned away from Fifer and plopped his shoulders against the truck. The soft hooting of an owl came from somewhere nearby. He stared through the night at the shadowy creek. The part that flowed through his land was much larger than it was downstream and looked more like a river. "I've been saving for years. I want to open a camp. Have a place for families to come to hike, fish, swim, decompress. It wouldn't be a big operation, just a special place for people to leave everything behind. I would be a fish guide, camp director—be hands on with everything." His voice grew stronger with enthusiasm. "I own a lot of the land across the creek. It is great for hiking. I'm going to build a few cabins on this side of the creek bank, set up a little shop so people can buy fishing gear and whatever they forget to pack, put a few picnic tables around, rent a few kayaks."

"You've really given this a lot of thought." Fifer leaned over, her arm next to his, marveling at an excitement in his voice she'd never heard before. "How long before you get the money to do it? I bet you could get a couple of investors to back you." She reached over and turned his face toward hers, his short whiskers prickling her palm. "This is really an amazing idea." She nodded toward the creek. "And you own the perfect place to make it happen. How far away are you financially from bringing it to life?"

"I'm there." Oscar's voice dropped down, the excitement ebbing away. "Dad gave me this land after he got married last year, so some of the money I was going to use to purchase the place could go toward the development. I just . . ." his words faded away.

"Oscar." Fifer pushed her palms into his cheeks. "You can do this. You have to do this. You have the money, the set-up, the business smarts, the—" she paused, her eyes darting around them. "The land smarts—or whatever you call it. You. Can. Do. This."

"Do you think so?"

"I *know* so." Fifer's enthusiasm bubbled out. "You could teach the kids some kind of outdoor class thing so the parents could have a little time to theirselves. Take them on a bug identification hunt, or whatever. Get coupons from your sister's restaurant and the pastry place if they wanted to stop through town on their way out at the end of their stay." She pulled her feet in and got up on her knees. "Oh, oh, oh! We could do some kind of crossover entertainment thing at the dinner theater." She poked Oscar in the arm. "What are you waiting for, man? This is a wonderful idea. You have everything you need. Go for it."

"I don't have everything." Oscar rose to his knees and

faced Fifer. He slipped his hand into his pocket and pulled something out, hiding it in his fist. "This isn't exactly how I planned to do this tonight."

Fifer's eyes cut down to Oscar's fist, then back to his face. Her eyes stretched wide and her mouth dropped open.

"There's one thing I don't have." Oscar flipped his hand over and opened his fingers, showing her the ring. "I don't have a partner." He picked up the ring between his fingers, his eyes down. "We can take as long of an engagement as you want, years if that's what it takes." He lifted his head, his eyes finding hers. "I know in my heart, in my everything, that you're the woman I want to spend the rest of my life with, Fifer McKenzie. Will you marry me?"

Fifer's heart pounded in her chest, and tears flooded her eyes. "Oscar, we've known each other a couple of months, and I'm, well."

Oscar leaned in and pressed his lips to Fifer's. He pulled back, his hands squeezing her shoulders. "You don't need to answer tonight. Especially after I dropped my plan of leaving my steady life for this." He tossed his head toward the creek without breaking eye contact. "It's a crazy scheme." He leaned in and touched his forehead to hers. "Don't say no, Fifer. At least not until you've given it some thought. I can be the man you want. I know I can."

"Oscar." Fifer swallowed, her words coming out in a whisper. "You are the man I want, the only man I want."

Oscar's arms wrapped around Fifer, squeezing the breath from her in his embrace. "Oops." He released her from the hug and looked over her shoulder. "I dropped the ring."

Fifer scooted out of his way and watched him grab his flashlight to search for the engagement ring. She wanted this, all of it. Oscar, the life he was planning, a future here in Red Creek, all of it. A tightness crept into her stomach. But how could she make it happen? She'd already determined she had to make things right with her past. If her father had gotten her out of manslaughter charges for her mother's death, like he claimed, she had to make all of that right somehow. She also had to unload all of this on Oscar.

"Found it." Oscar raised back up and held out the ring again. "Fifer?" He shined the flashlight in her face, then clicked it off. "What's wrong?"

"There's a lot about me you need to know."

"I don't care," Oscar said, cutting her off. "It doesn't matter who you were. All that matters is now. Us."

Fifer looked at his face. She loved that face. Her heart, her entire being, pulled against all the reasons to wait, to say no, to say not today. "Okay." She smiled softly. "I'll marry you, Oscar Robinson."

Oscar slipped the ring on her finger, then threw his head back and howled like a wolf. Laughter exploded from Fifer's chest. She would work it out somehow. Somehow, she would make amends with her past, get out from under her father's thumb, protect Oscar and this town from whatever the money-hungry man had planned. Somehow, she would do this without tearing out Oscar's heart.

"I love you, Fifer McKenzie." Oscar's voice dropped low, and he eased closer. "I love you, the future Fifer Robinson. You've made me the happiest man in Red Creek." He leaned down and kissed her.

She kissed him back, pushing away everything but that moment. When his lips left hers, Fifer put her hands on his shoulders, putting some distance between them. "Oscar. There are some things I need to tell you. Not tonight. But soon."

"Don't worry, Fifer." The moonlight cascaded down on Oscar's smiling face. "Whatever it is, we will handle it. I promise."

<h1>Chapter Twenty-Four</h1>

Ten days had passed since Oscar asked Fifer to marry him. Things had been great, better than great, actually, but she still hadn't opened up about what was bothering her. He wasn't a love-blind idiot, not completely, anyway. Something in her past was bothering her, and he'd bet his right arm it had to do with her father. He could get Odi to do a little more digging on the man. Knowing Odi, he probably already had, and was just waiting for him to ask for the information.

Oscar reached for his office phone, picked up the receiver, then put it back. No. He needed to do what he wanted Fifer to do with him. He needed to trust her to do what was right. He'd have to wait until she was ready to talk to him, then he'd help her. He grew still, thoughts lining up in his brain. She'd worked for her father ever since she was basically a teen. She had to know he was dirty. Like his father had drilled into his head over and over through the years, lost people acted like lost people. Why would you expect them to have the same moral compass as a believer in Christ? Now that Fifer was a believer, however, she would have to break away from the man. *Lord, please don't let her tackle that alone.*

He looked down at the papers in front of him, shuffling through the ones relating to different work projects. He pulled out a sheet and leaned back in his chair. He'd saved practically every penny since he'd started earning an income. He'd also invested, not wildly or recklessly, but in sure things. His portfolio had grown in a steady trickle. Now. Now the money was there to follow his dream. He could get a couple of backers and go wild with his idea, but that wasn't his style. He would start small, at least small by corporate standards, and let his venture grow. Build a few cabins, a store to sell things like bait and camping equipment, buy the boats, the kayaks, build a better road to the place, map out the hiking trails . . . .

Last year when his father deeded him the land, the idea of tackling this overwhelming task was so daunting. He'd told himself he needed to wait, that things weren't quite settled enough yet. Red Creek was growing, the tourism was trickling into town, but just wait until the venture was a sure thing. His postponement had been nothing but fear. Fear of failure, fear of being left with a pile of debt, no steady job, and being the laughingstock of Red Creek—being the Robinson that didn't make it.

Oscar tossed the paper on his desk. He picked up his phone and looked at a selfie he'd taken of him and Fifer in his truck with Festus wedged between them. Fifer believed he could do this; she thought he should do this. Her faith in him, seeing her excitement last week when he told her about his dream, and hearing her talk many times since then like his scheme was a certainty, like it was actually going to happen—her belief in him gave him courage. He had the ability to do this.

He'd started the ball rolling, looking into permits, revising the cost analysis he'd started a long time ago, setting up a timetable of when he could pull off his tie and hang up his accounting suit for the last time. It would take a year minimum to get the place open. This was another thing he needed to talk to Odi about. He needed his brother to help with all the legal things required to run an operation like this.

If things went according to his plan, before his camp became a reality, he'd be a married man. He stretched back in the chair and put his arms behind his head. He'd build their cabin a little further from where the rentals would be, maybe put a fence around their yard so she could do her yoga outside like she enjoyed. Oscar and Fifer Robinson. He liked the sound of that.

⁓⁓⁓

Fifer hung up her cell phone and rubbed her temples. The private investigator she'd hired last week had found plenty of dirt on her father. She'd specifically asked him to look into the businesses she'd help set up, the ones she'd willfully turned a blind eye to over the years. She'd set up the businesses, then turn them over to whomever her father sent to take over. She would walk away and leave the area to the poison she'd planted in the midst of the unsuspecting locals. She'd helped start up a seafood restaurant on the coast, a pizza place on the west side of the state near the Georgia border, and a convenience store in north Alabama on the Tennessee border. Over the years, those were the main projects she was entirely in charge of for months on end, getting the businesses started from the ground up.

The PI said the drug related arrests and complaints had

increased like clockwork the minute her father set up businesses in those towns. There was no traceable link to any of her father's businesses that could pinpoint his involvement, naturally. The convenience store on the Tennessee border, the first business she helped with several years ago, had been heavily investigated. Charges were brought up against the local man running the place. "Your father's name was mentioned several times, but he was not officially charged. He sold the company not long after, but I did a little more digging. He still owns the place, just under another name. Your father is as slick as a fox, Miss McKenzie. You'd better be careful."

"I will. Send me the paperwork on what you've found."

Fifer hung up her phone. The investigator hadn't told her anything she didn't already know about Louis McKenzie's character, but she had to do this. She didn't have a choice. She'd jumped into bed with the devil ten years ago when she let him do whatever he did to get her off of the manslaughter charges. Now, if she wanted to come clean, she'd have to face him. She could not let this town and these people be soiled by her father's plans.

She bit her lip as she pulled up the files the PI had emailed her. The restaurant on the coast was turning over a decent profit, but nothing amazing, just like the other places. Several articles from local newspapers, notes from police files, and other paperwork all painted a dismal picture. Her father was making some sort of pipeline for moving drugs through the state and covering it up with the businesses she helped set up.

Did she have enough information here to turn it in to the police? If she didn't, her father would retaliate against her with a vengeance, possibly harming Oscar in the process. She leaned back in her chair, pulled in a slow breath, and closed her eyes. "Lord, give me courage. Help me straighten this out and get out of my father's grip." She stayed like that for another minute, letting this new peace of knowing God was with her fill her.

She finally sat up and pulled up her father's files through the company's office website. She punched the last project she'd worked on, the one in Georgia, and started scrolling through the records. Everything looked fine to her eyes, but what did she expect? Louis McKenzie wouldn't leave anything incriminating out in the open for his employees, the ones who thought they were working for a normal real estate developer, to find. There were a couple of people in the business that were privy to her father's true colors, of this she was sure. Joseph DeCroux, the man her father sent to take over when she had the business foundation laid, was one. Unfortunately, there was no way to talk to him and keep her snooping secret. She couldn't ask him anything though. That man was loyal to her father. He would rat her out in a heartbeat.

Her brow furrowed. She typed out a new email to the PI. *Joseph DeCroux is my father's right-hand man. I'm sure he is involved in all of this and knows exactly what's going on. See what you can find out about him.*

A knock on her tiny office door made Fifer close her laptop. She looked up and smiled as Oscar walked in. "Are you about ready to go to the dinner theater?" Oscar asked, stepping closer. Fifer's smile broadened as he reached up and tugged at the knot in his tie. "They've gutted the place and got the electrical and plumbing up to code. You said you wanted to look at the plans one more time with the construction manager before we moved forward."

"Yes." Fifer pushed back from the desk and stood, drinking in Oscar's warm presence. "Let me run to the restroom and I'll meet you at your truck." She gathered her purse as he left. She had to get more information about her father. Something that would actually incriminate him and shut his operation down. She stepped into the bathroom a few feet down the hall from her office. The engagement ring on her finger gleamed up at her as she washed her hands. She needed to talk to her father. She had to take this bull by the horns. Oscar hadn't pushed her to tell him what was bothering her even though she knew he was aware something was upsetting her. She thought she had one of the best poker faces in the world, but not with him. He was waiting patiently for her to tell him what was going on. Her stomach churned as she looked at her reflection in the mirror. He trusted her, even knowing she was an alcoholic. He actually drove her to a lot of the meetings at the church. He knew liquor had once controlled her, knew about her monster, and yet he still believed in her.

Fifer dried her hands and tossed the brown paper towel in the trash near the bathroom door. Oscar had aided her in getting help with her internal monster, but she would not involve him in the monster that was her father. No, the thing that scared her more than her father, more than her past, more than going to jail for manslaughter, was that Oscar would get hurt by her dirty dealings. That would crush her. She would get out of this mess, break ties with Louis McKenzie completely, then tell Oscar about her past. It had to be that way. "Lord, please make it that way." She would gather what information she could and confront her father. She might even have to bluff her way through a few things, but she would not let him control her anymore.

What had Eric said at her last meeting? You can't have two masters. You have to submit your entire life, including your addiction, to God. It wasn't just a one time thing. It was a daily, hourly, minute by minute, thought by thought act of submission. She'd given Jesus control of her life, and there was no place for the dirty dealings of Louis McKenzie in it. She glanced at her reflection one more time, then left the bathroom, a tinge of fear mixing with her courage.

A couple of minutes later, Fifer tugged on her skirt, pulling it into place as she slid onto Oscar's truck seat. "Everything alright?" he asked, watching her buckle her seatbelt.

"Yes." Fifer smiled and set her purse on the floorboard. "I am just trying to get a few things straight with this project and my father and things. I'm a little distracted."

He picked up her hand and squeezed. "Need any help?"

"No. I am figuring it out."

"You don't have to figure it out alone, you know."

"I know." Fifer's eyes turned to the windshield. "I'll tell you if I need you."

"Promise?"

A twinge of guilt burned in Fifer's gut. "I promise." She wasn't lying to him. She could handle this herself. She had to handle this herself, for his sake.

The truck backed out of the parking lot, and they headed through Red Creek to the dinner theater. The little streets were about as busy as usual, with cars pulled in at the local businesses. A mother walked out of the barbershop with a little boy in tow with a fresh haircut. An old man in overalls headed into the hardware store, his wife at his side. The sound of the high school marching band practicing on the football field a few streets over filtered through the truck. Her father and his kind didn't belong here. She would not let Louis McKenzie poison Red Creek.

Chapter Twenty-Five

Things were progressing at the dinner theater, and the little town was getting excited. People were asking what the building was going to be, what jobs it would offer, what kind of entertainment would be there. It had been eight days since she'd first talked to the private investigator. Even though he'd gotten back with her about Joseph Decroux, her father's right-hand man, he hadn't uncovered anything concrete to connect her father to the increased drug problems that followed his entrance into the towns where he'd started businesses. Joseph Decroux had gotten out of prison twenty-five years ago with drug and assault charges, but nothing major since working with her father.

She looked at her cell phone lying beside her on the couch, almost eight o'clock. She had gotten in from the AA meeting that evening, then spent a little time in the backyard with Oscar and Festus. She'd put this off as long as she could. *God, give me the words to say and the courage to stand firm against him.* She punched her father's button and pulled her knees to her chest as her phone rang. "Father?"

"It looks like things are moving on down there. We may get the business up ahead of schedule."

That was her father. No hello, no how are you? Business, only business, always business. She would cut to the point, too. Make it short. "You're not moving into Red Creek. I want you to pull out."

"You what?" Louis McKenzie sounded surprised. Fifer imagined his eyebrows raising, his jaw slacking. She'd never gone against him on anything, not since her mother's death. Even when she'd looked into the accident on her own, she'd always buckled when he found out what she was doing, never questioned him about anything.

She swallowed. "I want." She paused, thinking about what she needed to say. "You are not moving your operation into Red Creek. I won't let you hurt this little town like you've done the others." The phone was silent. She'd managed to keep her voice steady and firm, even with her insides shaking. She braced herself for his onslaught.

"Fifer." His voice was pleasant now, like what a father should sound like, but hers never did. The man could change like a chameleon. "I heard you are drinking again. If you can't handle this job, I'll send someone else. I'll get you some help. It's okay to admit you're weak."

How did he know? Of course, he knew. Everyone knew she was going to AA. Bill Crestfield probably mentioned it on one of their calls. "I'm fine. I'm getting my own treatment. That is not the issue. I know you're running drugs. I know enough about you to get the feds to investigate you."

"You do, huh?" This voice was like ice. She knew this voice.

"I do. Leave Red Creek. Pull out and I'll keep quiet. If you don't . . . ." She let the words hang. It was an empty threat, at least for now. If he didn't pull out, she'd keep digging into his business, keep looking until she did find something. It was there, and she wouldn't give up until she found it.

Her father chuckled, a slimy sound. "You do realize that your name is all over everything in all these businesses. Why do you think I have you in this position? Certainly not because of your skill. If you go to the cops, the first person they will point a finger at is you, daughter, not me."

She pulled in a shaky breath. That was probably true, but so be it. "I won't back down. Either pull out, or I'm making another phone call first thing in the morning."

More silence. "Okay, Fifer." Louis McKenzie's voice sounded resigned, like he was the victim of a misconception. "If this is what you want, I'll do this for you. Get the money together, and I'll draw up the paperwork."

"Money?"

"Yes. If you really want me out of Red Creek, buy me out. That's how a legit business works. Despite your sudden lack of faith in me, I am still a legitimate businessman and need to think about the people depending on me in this project. If I pull out of this project now, it will jerk the rug out from under the Crestfield brothers. They only brought me into this deal because they didn't have the funds to cover it. If I pull out cold turkey, they will have to file bankruptcy."

Fifer frowned. What he said made sense. She had some money saved, but not nearly enough.

"Fifer? What's your answer?" Her father was polite now, knowing he'd manipulated her again, like he always did. "If you want to run with the big dogs, you have to get off the porch."

"I'll get back to you," Fifer said, her voice flat.

"You have twenty-four hours."

The phone went dead. What was she going to do? She tossed the phone on the couch and squeezed her hands into fists. She needed a drink. She felt the need just like she felt her fingernails cutting into her flesh. "Lord, help me," she whispered, tilting her head back. She grabbed her phone again and pulled up the scripture Eric had given her. 'He only is my rock and my salvation. My stronghold; I shall not be greatly shaken'.

She read through the Bible verses until she got to the one she was looking for. "I waited patiently for the Lord; He turned to me and heard my cry. He lifted me out of the slimy pit, out of the mud and mire; He set my feet on a rock and gave me a firm place to stand." Fifer wiped a tear from her eye. "God, give me Your strength and wisdom. Show me how to fix this. Show me how to not hurt the ones I care about."

Oscar's head rested on the arm of the sofa, his long legs stretching across the cushions, his feet hanging off the other end. Festus lay on top of him, and Oscar stroked his head. The dog's relaxing contentment of just being near his master gave Oscar comfort. The ball was rolling. He'd talked to Odi about his plans, and his lawyer-brother was researching what permits and other documents needed to be obtained to start the physical process of turning his piece of Red Creek into a recreational camp for the public. He'd tightened up his business plan and was sure he could make this work. In one more year, he could throw away his suit and tie forever.

Festus raised his head and woofed softly. "What's up, boy? You need to go out?" The dog jumped down from the sofa, using Oscar's stomach as his springboard. "Oof, Festus." Oscar sat up. "Warn me next time before you do that."

Festus ignored Oscar and trotted to the front door, wagging his tail. A second later, a soft knock sounded. Oscar looked at the nearby wall clock. It was eight-forty-five. Fifer was usually in bed by this time, but it had to be her. Nobody else made Festus wiggle like that. He opened the door and watched as Fifer squatted down and hugged Festus. Would their kids have red hair or black hair? It would have to be curly. There was no way around that.

Fifer stood and leaned onto Oscar, her head laying on his chest, not speaking. He wrapped his arms around her shoulders. "Hey." His soft voice caressed the top of her head. Something had been bothering her for the last couple of weeks. Maybe she was ready to talk. He stroked her back, much like he stroked Festus earlier, only this time he was the comfort giver. "Come on in."

She pulled away and walked over to the sofa, shoulders slumped, feet dragging. He shut the front door and followed, watching her sit on one corner. Festus crawled into her lap and snuggled, covering most of her body. She wrapped her arms around the dog like she was drowning in the ocean and he was a life raft.

"You want to talk about it?" Oscar set on the other end of the couch, giving her space.

Fifer's chin rested on the top of Festus's head; her eyes cast down. "I'm trying to fix this mess, but instead of making it better, I think I might be making it worse."

Oscar leaned forward and pushed back Fifer's fiery mane cascading over her face. "Let me in, Fifer. We are partners now. You can share whatever's going on with me."

Fifer turned her face to Oscar, her eyes glassy with unshed tears. "When I was seventeen, I killed my mother." She stopped, her eyes searching Oscar's face.

Oscar's brow pulled down. Of everything in the world he

expected her to say, that had not been anywhere on his radar. "How?"

Fifer rubbed her lips together. "I was drinking. We were in the car together. I don't remember what happened. At least I don't remember it correctly." Her forehead wrinkled. "My mother had been drinking too, but she came to pick me up from a bar. We wrecked, and my mother was killed. I don't really remember any of it except a few flashes. I had a concussion and some broken bones. I woke up in the hospital, my father telling me what happened."

Tears started to pour from Fifer's eyes. Oscar leaned forward and pulled her into his lap. Festus shuffled around and curled up on her other side. "I'm so sorry," Oscar whispered, letting her cry on his chest.

"My father sent me straight from the hospital to rehab. He said that was the only way to keep me out of prison. He said if I'd sober up, come to work for him, and carry my weight, he'd make sure the manslaughter charges disappeared."

Oscar frowned. Fifer's head continued to lie against him. She had been seventeen, a minor. Would they have tried her as an adult in what was obviously a terrible accident? Especially if both of the people in the car had been drinking? Now was not the time for the questions, but he would be looking into this. He didn't trust Louis McKenzie any farther than he could spit. There had to be a way to look into what happened and make sure her father hadn't used the situation to control his daughter.

Fifer lifted her head and wiped her eyes. "I came out of rehab and went to work for my father. I took college classes and earned a business degree all at the same time. Ever since then, I've been part of my father's business."

"You were young, Fifer. Still a kid, really. It doesn't seem like you had much of a choice."

Fifer scooted over and wiped the back of her hand across

her eyes. "I guess not at first, but not for ten years. I should have taken responsibility for what I did a long time ago, but I didn't. Now." She blinked her eyes and looked down at Festus. Oscar waited silently. She slowly looked up. "Now I'm in such a deep mess. And I'm dragging you and this sweet town into it with me."

Oscar's heart squeezed in his chest. She looked so broken, so vulnerable. Nothing like the woman he'd first met in that boardroom. He wanted to pull her in and protect her from everything and everyone. He wanted to throttle Louis McKenzie for letting her carry this guilt for all these years. "Tell me."

"I have always known my father was underhanded." Fifer rubbed her hands down her face, emotional fatigue playing on her features. "I've heard rumors, conversations that stopped when I came in the room, signs that things were not what they seemed, but I always looked the other way. Not out of concern for my father." She looked down again, her fingers running along Festus's head. "There's no love lost between us. It was simply self-preservation. But that day you took me to see Eric." She lifted her face and let out a puff of air. "The day I gave my life to Christ, I knew things had to change. So . . ." Her face tilted upward, eyes searching the ceiling. "Tonight, I called my father and told him he could not bring his business to Red Creek. He pulls out or I will turn him in to the police or feds or whoever will listen."

"What's he involved in? What did he say?"

"See." Fifer sniffed and looked again at Oscar. "That's the thing. I'm positive he's using these businesses I helped start to sell drugs, but in reality, I don't have any proof of this." She shrugged. "I was bluffing."

Oscar looked at her red-rimmed eyes, swollen from crying. No wonder she'd been acting distracted. She had to be one of the strongest people he'd ever met. She'd gone through all of that alone and without turning back to drinking. "What did he say?"

"He said I could buy him out. If he pulls out his backing, the Crestfields will go bankrupt."

"I was afraid of that." Oscar's eyes narrowed. "I tried to talk to Bill about going into business with Louis McKenzie, but he assured me everything was fine."

"So, you think my father is being honest about this? The bankruptcy part?"

"Probably." Oscar rubbed his hand along his jaw. "When does he want the money?"

"In twenty-four hours." Fifer leaned back against the sofa. "He doesn't think I'll come up with it. I'm sure tomorrow evening he'll fire me and continue on with his plans." Her lips puckered. "Or who knows? He may fire me and pull out anyway, just to spite me." She looked at Oscar, defeat weighing her down. "Either way, I have let my father loose on your town, and the outcome will not be good."

"First of all." Oscar pulled her back closer to him. "It's not my town—it's our town. We are getting married—one day— and I'm assuming we will live together here, in Red Creek." She nodded her head against his shoulder, not looking up. "Good. Next, I have almost enough to buy him out, and I can get the rest."

"Oscar, no." Fifer's head jerked up. "I can't let you do that. Your plans . . ."

"My plans include marrying you, Fifer McKenzie, and raising our future kids right here in this peaceful little town. Everything else doesn't really matter." Festus stood and stepped over Fifer and licked Oscar in the face. "And keeping this crazy dog happy. That goes without saying."

Chapter Twenty-Six

Oscar texted Bill Crestfield and told him he wouldn't be in the office today, but available by phone if they needed him. He had not missed a single day of work until Fifer dropped into his life. Before she came along, his life had been in such a routine it could almost be called a rut. Now she was stretching him, for sure, but he was all in. When he put his old dream of a bachelor life on the banks of Red Creek next to his new dream of Fifer and a brood of curly headed, strong-willed kids . . . dream number two won every time.

Oscar opened his computer and pulled up his bank account. His fingers raked down his cheek. He had no regrets where Fifer was concerned. Zero. The problem was, how was he going to fulfill last night's promise? He could wipe out his savings completely and still be over one hundred thousand dollars short. McKenzie hadn't invested the amount of money he told Fifer last night, not if he had put up half the capital like Bill Crestfield had told Oscar. No, McKenzie was padding his offer to make more cash. They would take over his share of the investment with the majority of the money, but a lot would go directly into the other man's pocket. The under-handed businessman probably gave Fifer an amount he thought would make it impossible for her to buy him out. Either way, it didn't matter. Oscar had to get the man's influence out of Red Creek—and more importantly—out of Fifer's life.

He closed his laptop and scooped his keys off the coffee table. It was almost nine. His father should be at his store, but if he wasn't, he'd track him down. Last night, after Fifer left and after a lot of praying, Oscar had come up with a plan. He'd borrow the rest of the money from his parents and put up his land on Red Creek as collateral. It had been his dad's land to begin with, but he'd broken everything up after he gotten married last year. He'd deeded all the kids their sections, keeping only a couple of acres where he built his new house.

Oscar pulled up in front of the junk store a few minutes later and looked at the place. His mother's influence was definitely showing. No doubt she'd hung the clear party lights on the overhang across the storefront. The glass windows and door were actually clean, not the smoky brown they'd been for decades, and the biggest improvement, at least in his opinion, was the parking lot. It was smooth with visible stripes, not a pothole in sight.

The doorbell jingled as Oscar and Festus walked in. One of his mother's songs, from back when she was making the billboard in country music, played in the background as he headed to the counter in the rear of the store.

"You two set a date yet?" Orville stepped out from a nearby aisle. "Your momma is itching to help plan the wedding."

"No." Oscar leaned on the counter. Festus sat obediently at his feet. "Have you got a minute? I need to talk to you."

"Sure, son." Orville's jovial tone dropped and mirrored the concern on Oscar's face. "Come back to the office." The two men and the dog went around the counter to the little office tucked in the back. "Have a seat and tell me what's on your mind."

"Fifer's father, the man who's putting up money with the Crestfields to build the dinner theater, is not a man we want in Red Creek."

"I see." Orville Robinson reached in his pocket and pulled out a piece of butterscotch candy. "What is it about him that makes you feel this way?"

"Fifer feels certain he is a drug dealer, and he plans to use the dinner theater to bring that sort of thing into Red Creek." Oscar's shoulders fell back in the little wooden chair and he rubbed his palms together. "Dad, if you could see how he treats Fifer—it's terrible. I won't go into details because she needs to tell her own story, but the man is total slime." He sat forward, pulling himself up straight in the chair. "I want him out of her life and out of this town. Permanently."

Orville stopped opening his candy and looked at Oscar for a couple of seconds. "Is this what Fifer wants? To be cut off from her family?"

"Yes, sir." Oscar nodded. "She told me last night about what she thinks he will do when he comes into Red Creek. She would turn him in to the law, but she doesn't have any proof." Oscar's words rushed out. "But he said if she'd buy him out, he'd cut ties with the Crestfields. And more important, Fifer could cut ties with him, get out from under his thumb."

"He wants her to pay him off." Orville's lips pushed flat, and he slowly rubbed his hand across his chin, his eyes studying his son. "Alright." He slapped his hands on the table, and Festus woofed in response. "How much will it take?"

Oscar blew out a breath. He'd felt certain his father would

help. Even so, it was good to actually hear him offer. Oscar gave him the amount he needed. "I will put the land you deeded me up for collateral if you can loan me the money." His voice slowed as what he was asking sunk in. "And if it won't put you and Momma in any kind of hard situation financially."

"I don't want your land back, son. I gave it to you, and it's yours. And don't worry about me and your momma. We have a buck or two stuck back." He grinned. "I guess I'll be part owner of that theater you're building." His grin broadened. "My only stipulation is you let your mother perform every once in a while. She would love that."

Oscar's head tilted to the side as he stared at his father. "I hadn't given that part a lot of thought. I guess I'll be owning part of the Red Creek dinner theater."

"Son." Orville picked up the candy he had laid on the table and slipped it into his mouth. "You understand that Louis McKenzie may not follow through with his promise. Men like him don't get where they are because of their honest dealings."

"He'll keep his end of the deal." Oscar's eyes narrowed. "Fifer . . . knows things."

"Be careful. When you corner a wild dog, they usually come at you baring their fangs."

"Don't worry." Oscar's jaw hardened. "If he wants a fight, he'll get one. Fifer—and Red Creek—are too important to let him drag them down to his level."

"That doesn't seem like nearly enough money to buy the man out." Doubt filled Orville's tone. "Are you sure that's all you need?"

"I." Oscar's eyes looked away from his father's scrutiny. "I'm putting up the rest. Like I said, I'll be part owner of a dinner theater."

"I would ask you if you're sure this is what you want to do, but I understand. When the right woman gets in your heart, your head and everything else follows along."

Oscar looked back at his father. "Thanks for understanding."

"If you need me, call me." Orville pushed his chair back. "I'll talk to Lucy and get the money to you this afternoon." He grinned. "I still have my shotgun behind my truck seat. If Fifer's dad needs a little persuasion to do the right thing, you let me know."

Oscar stood and smiled. His father was only partially joking. He wouldn't shoot anyone, but he would defend his family or die trying. Of that, Oscar was certain. "It won't come to that." *I hope.*

By lunchtime, Oscar's father had called. Oscar left Festus at home for this trip since Festus wasn't allowed in the bank. He had a few other errands to run as well. He and his father met at the bank and transferred the money from Orville's account to Oscar's. "I still can't believe how all of us kids worried about you and thought you were struggling for money for all those years."

Orville grinned as they walked out of the bank. "None of you ever hurt for anything money could buy as a kid. And what you thought after you were grown, well, that's none of my concern, is it?"

Oscar chuckled. "I guess not." They continued across the parking lot to their trucks parked side by side. "I know part of why you kept your wealth hidden was to teach us to value work and things," Oscar said, looking at his father. "But I get the feeling there was more to it than that. You've changed so much since Mom came back."

"Yeah." Orville squinted his eyes, his playful grin turning to a contemplative stare. "I think I was scared that if you kids didn't think I needed you around, that you would leave too. I didn't realize it at the time . . . or did it with that intention, but looking back, I believe that was behind at least part of it."

"And now?"

"Now I know that I have to trust all of you to the Lord's care. I've got to be the best man I can be, but I'm not in control. God is." Orville grinned again. "Your momma is head over heels in love with being part owner of the dinner theater. I told her not to blab this around, but I have to tell you, she doesn't quite understand the concept of a silent partner. It's sort of like telling Owen a secret."

Oscar thanked his father again and drove the short distance to Odi's law office.

"Back so soon?" Odi looked up from behind his desk. "You will have your fishing camp up and going in six months if you keep up this pace."

"I'm not here about the camp." Oscar sat down in the leather chair across from his brother. "Actually, I guess I am. You can stop working on all of that for now. I'm not opening it up after all."

Odi's eyebrows raised. "What happened? You were so gung-ho yesterday."

"I'm buying into the dinner theater instead."

"Dinner theater?" Odi threw his head back and laughed. "You?"

Oscar scowled. "Yes, me. Now quit your laughing and listen to me." He filled Odi in on what Fifer told him last night. "I need an iron-clad, unbreakable contract, so that once

Louis McKenzie receives the money, there is no way he can get back into the deal. No loopholes that allow him to have anything to do with the theater."

"I can do that." Odi picked up a pencil and scratched something on a piece of paper. "Of course, there's no way to keep him from buying something else, but we can make sure he doesn't have anything to do with this establishment."

"There's one thing I can do." Oscar leaned back in the chair. "If Fifer is okay with the idea, I'm going to make sure Louis McKenzie's name and what he really stands for is known around this town. If the Crestfields and Gordon Blue and other money people in this town know Louis McKenzie's true colors, we can work together to keep him and his type of dealings out."

"Whoa-hoa. Slow down, cowboy." Odi leaned back in his chair. "You start doing that and folks around here will have you running for public office."

"Not me." Oscar frowned. "As soon as all of this is said and done, I'm going back to minding my own business. I just wish there was a way to do something legally to guarantee the man would stay away from Fifer, too."

"Does she have a reason to get a restraining order against him?"

"No. To my knowledge, he's never done anything physical to her. He's just made sure she was filled with enough guilt to keep her under his control." Oscar stood up from his chair. "When can you have the contract ready? He's calling Fifer tonight, and I want her to be able to tell him everything is set to go."

"Tomorrow."

"Good. We may have to drive to Birmingham to get this done." Oscar paused and looked down at his brother. "If we do, can you watch Festus for me? I don't like leaving him alone overnight."

"Sure." Odi stood. "Just let me know." He followed Oscar to the door. "But I have a question."

"What's that?"

"When you and Fifer go on your honeymoon, is Festus going too?"

"Well, yeah."

Chapter Twenty-Seven

Fifer looked up and down the main street of Red Creek. A few stars twinkled overhead, mixing with only a sliver of moonlight. Her car barely moved as she took in the quiet calmness of the small town. She was on her way back from her AA meeting. Normally, with the long summer days, she would get home before it was completely dark, but tonight's sharing and praying times had run long. Mr. Bob from the pastry shop had noticed her new ring. After the meeting, he asked with a conspirator's grin who the lucky man was. "I thought you two were getting a little cozy," he'd said, giving her a hug.

She didn't mind the delay at all. She was postponing the call to her father for as long as she could. She wasn't scared of him, not now that she had Oscar at her side. That wasn't it. If he turned her in to the police for being the driver of the car in the crash, that was no more than what she was going to do herself. She had no idea what the outcome of the situation would be, but she had to come clean, had to get out from under the oppressing guilt of the secret. She'd confessed it to

God, confessed it to the man she loved. Now she had to make it right.

The party lights strung along a few of the store fronts twinkled as her car crept by. The car top was down, and a warm breeze blew across her face, bringing the smell of charcoal and seared meats from a barbeque from somewhere not too far away. Instead of driving directly home, she drove over to the theater. The place should be dark this time of the evening, and the building was, but a beat-up old truck was backed in front of it, a truck she recognized. She pulled in beside it and walked around to the tailgate, squinting to see exactly who was there. Orville and Lucy Robinson sat, holding hands, each sipping a Coke.

"Hello, Fifer." Lucy smiled and shined a tiny penlight in her direction. "I asked Orville to drive me over after supper and let me see the place. I can't tell you how excited I am to actually be a part of opening a dinner theater in our little town."

Redness crept up Fifer's cheeks, and she was thankful for the cover of darkness to hide her surprise and embarrassment. Her future in-laws bailing her out of a financial debacle was not something she was proud of, and she sure wasn't expecting them to be happy about it.

"About that." Fifer cleared her throat. "I want you both to know how thankful." She paused. People said those words so many times for so many things. They didn't seem to be enough. "I will repay the money. You have no idea how much this means to me."

"Honey." Lucy slid off the tailgate and passed her Coke to Orville. "We are investing. You're not going to pay us back. Sink or swim, we're in this little venture together now." She wrapped her thin arm around Fifer's waist and squeezed. "But don't you worry, we are going to make this place a blazing success. Orville said I can't say anything to anybody about it yet, but as soon as I can, I have a million ideas for the place I want to talk to you about. I am thinking Tex-Mex for the menu."

"She's a little enthusiastic," Orville said, his voice carrying through the near darkness. "How did things go with your father?"

Fifer wanted to lean her head over onto the shorter woman like she would a real mother, but she didn't. She pulled in a deep breath. "I have to call him to set up a meeting when I get home. Oscar said a contract for the sale-out will be ready by tomorrow." A shudder flooded down her spine. "Everything should go smoothly, but with my father, you never know."

Lucy's arm tightened around Fifer. "You are not alone in this, dear. You've got Oscar and the rest of the Robinsons coming alongside you, and even more important than that, you have the Lord."

"I know." A tear trickled down Fifer's cheek. "I've been doing things on my own for so long that having people help me is sort of odd."

"Believe it or not," Lucy said, "I know exactly how that feels." She took Fifer's hand and stepped closer to Orville, taking his, too. "Pray for this sweet girl, Orville."

Orville took Lucy's hand in his, then, right there in front of the dinner theater in the dark of night, Orville prayed for peace and strength and God's hand to guide Fifer in all she was facing. Fifer listened in awe. What was it going to be like to be a part of this special family?

"Now." Orville released her hand. "You better get on about your business."

Fifer hugged both of the Robinsons and got back in her car. She turned toward her little duplex where Oscar was no doubt waiting for her. When she'd come in from work, he'd filled her in on his day of gathering the money from his parents and talking to his brother about the contract. He'd talked to the Crestfield brothers about the buyout of Louis McKenzie's share of the project. The brothers were very skeptical and wanted to call her father themselves until Oscar told them he and his family would be buying the man out. They had happily gone along then, not so much because they wanted to be in business with Oscar or Orville, but the idea of having Lucy Robinson, the country music singer on board, had appealed to them a lot. He'd handled all of it so far, and he would call her father if she wanted him to. He'd offered several times already. She'd turned him down. She had to do this, had to be the one to tell the man she was out for good.

The living room lights on Oscar's side of the duplex shone through his window as she pulled up. A shadow stood from the rocker on the front porch, and Festus bounded off the steps and met her as she got out of the car. She had to be the one calling her father, but she didn't have to do it alone. *Thank you, God, for these people, this town, especially Oscar.*

Oscar stood beside Fifer, her hand in his, his eyes watching her face as she pulled up her father's number on the phone. For a woman, she had a grip of steel. He wiggled his fingers, and she loosened slightly, never looking in his direction. Her eyes focused on the phone, almost like she could see the man on the other end. She'd put him on speaker at Oscar's request.

"His language can get rough when things don't go his way," Fifer said, biting her bottom lip like she often did when she was unsure.

"That's okay," Oscar said. "If he gets ugly, I don't have a problem shutting him up."

"So, you finally decided to call me back." Louis McKenzie's smug voice came from the phone, now lying on the coffee table.

"I have the money and the contract for you to pull out of the deal." Fifer's voice was all business, even though Oscar's fingers were slowly turning purple from her grip.

"You do, huh?" Surprise oozed from her father's voice.

"I do. I can drive to Birmingham tomorrow, and we can get this done."

"No." McKenzie paused. "Tomorrow's no good. Make it Monday."

Fifer's eyebrows raised, and she glanced over at Oscar. "Okay. I'll be at your office on Monday at one." The phone went dead. No goodbye, no, I'll see you then, nothing. Fifer released Oscar's hand and wrapped her arms around his neck. "I can't believe how easy that was."

"It was. Something. That's for sure." Oscar shook out his hand to get the blood flowing again, then returned Fifer's hug. "Your father is about as rude as they come."

"Oh, that was nothing. He was on his good behavior." Fifer pulled back and smiled up at Oscar. "He probably thought I had a cop or someone in the room trying to catch him in saying something he shouldn't." Festus hopped up on the sofa beside them, then wedged his head and shoulders between them. "Hey, boy." Fifer stepped back and wrapped her arms around the dog. "You need some loving, too?"

Oscar watched Fifer sit down and pet Festus, her demeanor so different now than it had been a few seconds ago when she was on the phone. His chest tightened. That part of her life would soon be behind her. As long as he had a breath in his body, he would protect her from that man.

Fifer looked up at Oscar. "Are you okay?"

"Yeah." Oscar smiled. "Why?"

"You had a funny look on your face."

"I'm just glad all of this is almost over." He sat down on the other side of Festus. The dog leaned over and licked him in the face. He shoved him away and laughed. "I have some ice cream in the fridge. Why don't we celebrate this moment?"

"That sounds wonderful."

They walked into the kitchen, and Oscar took the butter pecan ice cream from his freezer. "Want to eat it in the back-yard or in the living room?" Oscar pulled a couple of bowls from the cabinet and started dipping.

"Back yard, please." Fifer's arms reached around his flat stomach from behind, her chin resting between his shoulder blades. "I want you to do something."

"What's that?" Oscar's heart pounded, feeling the curves of Fifer's body against his back.

"I want you and Festus to go camping at Red Creek this weekend like old times."

Oscar dropped the ice cream scoop in the container and turned to face Fifer. "Why don't you go with us? I'll set you up in your very own tent and everything."

"No." Fifer shook her head. "I know how much you sacrificed to get me away from my father."

"But."

"No." Fifer raised her finger to Oscar's lips. "Listen to me. I have a plan." Her lips turned up in a slow smile, and Oscar's heart revved up a few more notches. "You and Festus go to Red Creek this weekend, and I'll do a little shopping. On Monday, while we're in Birmingham, let's go ahead and get married before we go see my father."

"Elope?" Oscar's voice dropped low and heat filled his chest. "Are you sure?"

"Very sure. We can come back to Red Creek as husband

and wife. And." She placed a quick kiss on his lips and stepped away, her eyes sparkling. "Live happily ever after."

Oscar stepped forward, following her like she was a magnetic force. His body longed for her to be next to him like she was before.

Fifer held out her hand, keeping him at arm's length. "What do you think? Is it a deal?"

"Definitely."

Oscar pushed in closer, but Fifer took another step backwards. Reaching behind her, she opened the back door, stepped through, and pulled it shut behind her. She pushed her face against the glass part of the door and laughed. "Don't forget our ice cream."

Oscar frowned. Ice cream? He blinked, trying to control the sudden flow of emotions overtaking his body and his brain. Oh yeah, they were getting ice cream. He smiled at Fifer, then turned back to the counter. He grabbed the two bowls and hurried to the backdoor, Festus on his heels. Yes, eloping was a splendid plan, an excellent plan. But it was going to be a torturously long weekend on Red Creek.

Chapter Twenty-
Eight

Oscar waved at Fifer through the truck window as he
backed out of the driveway. He had been smiling
like a schoolboy, wearing a goofy grin all day long.
He couldn't help it. By this time Monday, he would be a
married man. Married to the gorgeous red head waving to him
and Festus, her smile as big as his. Sure, the idea of working as
an accountant for the next however long it took appealed to
him about as much as eating rocks, but it didn't matter. If he
got to come home every day to Fifer, he could take just about
anything.

Besides, who knew what the future held? Unexpected
changes happened. The past few months were proof of that.
His life had rolled along one day like the next for years, then
wham. Fifer stepped in and flipped his world upside down. He
would be part owner of a dinner theater soon. He didn't have
a clue how the front end of that sort of thing worked, but his
brother Owen and his mother did. Not only was his life
changing, but his little town was evolving, and now, because
Fifer was taking a stand, the change would be for the better.

He cruised through the town and looped by the theater.

The workers were packing up and leaving for the day. Several waved and called greetings as he crept by. The building was changing rapidly, with new improvements daily. A new marquee was above the door. The bricks had been pressure cleaned, the cracked glass replaced. Even from the outside, you could tell it was not the same old building.

Oscar continued out of town, his mind wandering through the past and wondering about the future. He wasn't in a hurry to get where he was going like he used to be. He wasn't running from his present anymore. He could be happy anywhere today, as long as Fifer was happy. Out of town, a couple of vehicles sped around him, probably in a hurry to get home, or maybe making a weekend trip to the coast. He didn't care. He cranked up the radio as the announcer described a new and upcoming voice making a splash in Nashville. Ori Robinson's voice filled the truck, and Oscar chuckled. Little brother was chasing his star. Good for him.

Oscar's truck rounded the curve near his turn onto the gravel road and a shiny black car came into view from the opposite direction, driving toward Red Creek. Oscar turned on his blinker and waited for it to pass. He stared at the man behind the wheel as he went by and looked at his license plate in his rearview mirror. Alabama plates. That didn't tell him much, but still, the guy looked familiar. He watched the car disappear out of sight then turned onto the gravel road and stopped. He'd seen several pictures of Louis McKenzie over the past day or two. He'd researched the man online after Fifer talked to him Wednesday night, but only found a few pictures of him shaking hands with other businessmen or the local mayor or other fluff. The thing he noticed the most was the guy's red hair—just like the man who'd passed a few seconds before.

Oscar's throat tightened. *Don't panic. Lots of men have red hair.* He picked up the phone and punched Fifer's number as the words crawled through his head.

"Hey." Fifer's cheerful voice eased the clenching of Oscar's stomach. "You missing me already?"

"Yeah." Oscar forced his voice to be calm. He was overreacting. No need to panic Fifer. "What're you doing?"

"I'm eating a taco, then I'm going to my meeting. You know, your mother called me a while ago. She thinks the dinner theater should serve Mexican food. There's not a Mexican place in Red Creek. What do you think?"

"Makes sense." Oscar's shoulders relaxed, and he started down the gravel road. "I love Mexican food almost as much as I love you."

"Your mom has a lot of good ideas." Fifer paused. "Hold on a second. Someone's at the door."

Oscar hit his truck brakes again, listening intently to his phone. Shuffling noises, the front door opening. "What are you doing here?" Fifer's tone was icy, the voice she used with only one person. He listened over his heart pounding in his ears, but couldn't make out what was being said. The phone went dead.

Oscar jerked his truck into reverse and backed down the gravel road at breakneck speed. He wheeled onto the pavement, rocks slinging everywhere, and raced back toward town. He surely was overreacting again. The man probably decided to move some things around, then drove in today to get all of this over with. Oscar shoved the gas pedal to the floor and took the curve on two wheels, slamming Festus against the passenger's door. His head pounded as the scenery flew by. Why had he left her alone? Stupid, stupid, stupid. The man was dangerous. Odi had warned him, Fifer feared him. Yet they had taken him at his word last night like naïve four year olds. *Lord, please let me be wrong. Please let me find Fifer talking to my dad or Bill Crestfield, or anybody. Anybody besides that father of hers.*

An eternity later, he pulled onto the side of the road in front of their duplex. Cold sweat ran down his spine. The black car, the same black car he'd passed a few minutes ago, was parked in his spot. Festus let out a low, menacing growl. "I know, boy." Oscar opened the truck door, and the dog bolted over him and made a beeline for Fifer's door, jumping up and pawing to get inside, something he'd been trained not to do.

Oscar ran to Fifer's door and threw it open. "Fifer?" He yelled her name, eyes taking in the empty living room. Festus flew through the door and up the stairs, his barks filling the duplex.

Oscar followed the dog's breakneck speed, stumbling over the coffee table as he hurried by. A shot rang out as he reached the bottom of the stairs and his entire body clenched. He hurried up the stairs, but time seemed to warp into slow motion. "Fifer!"

"What are you doing here?" Fifer felt the blood draining from her face. She should have known last night's phone call had been too easy.

"Taking care of business, darling." Louis McKenzie's lips spread to a wicked grin as he reached for her cell phone. Fifer pulled her hand back. "Reconsider, girl," Louis said, waving the little pistol in his other hand toward her gut. She handed him the phone. He switched it off and dropped it in his pants pocket. "That's better."

"What are you doing here?" Fifer repeated the question. Her mind raced, trying to figure out how to get away from the man who'd controlled her entire adult life. Her keys were in her purse upstairs. Pepper spray was on the keychain. If she could catch him off guard long enough to spray him, she could get away. "Are you going to shoot me?"

"Not here." Louis McKenzie smirked. "Well, not unless I have to." He waved the gun toward the living room. "Get that money you said you have. We're going home, then I'll deal with you."

"What's going to happen to me?" Fifer didn't actually have the check for the buyout. Oscar did. It was his money after all. Her father didn't need to know that. She'd taken a kickboxing combo self-defense class several years ago, and she was a little taller than her father. Could she gut kick him and get out the door before he shot her? There was no doubt he would shoot her. She was a tool to him. Now that she wasn't a useful tool, he would do away with her.

"Once I get the money, we'll head back to Birmingham. I'll call the Crestfield man on Monday and tell him I've changed my mind about pulling out. I'll explain that the problem all along was you. You weren't cutting it. I've pulled you out, and I'm sending someone else to take over. Nobody here will question my decision. Nobody in Birmingham will think a thing about you going overseas to live. You will just fade away."

"How can you kill your own daughter? I know you don't love me, but I'm your flesh and blood."

"You're my flesh and blood alright, but not *my* daughter." A glint of pure hatred blazed from Louis McKenzie's eyes. "Have you even looked at yourself? The only thing we have in common is the hair. All of us McKenzie's have the hair. You are Robert's kid, through and through. Your mother wanted to have her cake and eat it too, but I showed her."

"Uncle Robert?" Fifer's eyes stretched wide. Her father's kid brother had died in a hunting accident when she was six. She only had a few memories of him. They all were of him with her mother, never her father. The sudden realization dawned on her as Louis McKenzie's words sunk in. "He was my father?"

"Like I said, look in the mirror." Louis ran his hand up and down in front of him. "My kid brother was tall and slim like you, and looked more like Mamma than Pop. Your mother started fooling around with him shortly after we got married. It took me a while to catch on, but when I did, I took care of it. She was only after my money."

Fifer tried to focus, tried to think of something to say, but no words came. This man was not her father? Several emotions pushed in from all directions. Anger, confusion, sadness. And relief. She pulled in a deep breath and pushed her shoulders back. "You killed him when you found out about the affair. Then you made Mother's life miserable."

"Why not?" Louis shrugged a shoulder. "They betrayed me. Nobody betrays me and gets away with it. They deserved what they got." His eyes roamed the room, then returned to Fifer. "We've wasted enough time on this. Where's the check?"

"Upstairs," Fifer said, her mind still reeling with the revelation of her parentage. She swallowed and looked toward the stairs, forcing herself to focus. "I'll go get it."

"*We* will go get it." Louis waved the gun in that direction. "I'm not stupid, Fifer. I imagine you have your own gun up there. Make no mistake. I will shoot you right here if you provoke me and not bat an eye."

"I bet you will," Fifer mumbled under her breath. She crossed the room and moved up the stairs, Louis McKenzie right behind her. She pulled in a deep breath. "You're wrong, you know."

"About what?"

"The people around here will wonder where I've gone. They'll miss me and come looking for me."

Louis McKenzie's wheezy laugh came from behind her.

"Don't kid yourself. You leave today, and by Friday they won't remember your name. And if there are a few that ask questions, I'll take care of that." They reached the top of the stairs, and he leaned against the rail. "Hold on a second, and let me catch my breath."

Fifer slipped her engagement ring from her finger before she turned around. The last thing she needed was her father to go after Oscar. "You're wrong. I've changed while I was here. I'm not who I was, and I've made friends."

"You've gone soft. That's what you've done." He stood up straight. "Alright. Find that check, and let's get on the road."

She stepped through her bedroom doorframe; Louis McKenzie so close behind her she could feel his labored breathing on her neck. The sound of the front door opening came from below, followed by Oscar calling her name, along with a menacing bark from Festus. Fifer whirled around as Festus reached the top of the stairs and jumped toward Louis McKenzie, his teeth snarling. Her father turned toward the charging dog and Fifer lunged to grab the gun in his hand, but she was too late.

"No!" Fifer's scream cut through the air as Festus fell to the ground. She dove into the hall where the dog lay, blood turning the golden hair on his hip crimson red. She landed on all fours, forgetting her father still had the gun. Oscar appeared at the top of the stairs and flew through the air above her head, tackling Louis McKenzie. The two men crashed through her bedroom door and landed on the floor nearby. The gun let out an explosive shot again behind her. Festus flinched at the sound, and her heart leapt in her chest. The dog wasn't dead. Not yet anyway. She turned and looked behind her, her shaking torso hitting the floor, her vision blurred with tears.

"Fifer." Oscar's voice barked from a few feet away. "I've got him," he said, his knee planted between Louis McKenzie's shoulder blades, the man's arms pinned behind him. The older man puffed and wheezed like a locomotive but didn't say a word. Oscar reached down and slid the gun in her direction. "Do something with this, and call the cops or the sheriff or somebody."

"Oscar." Fifer's voice shook along with her fingers. She picked up the gun and set it away from the door. "He shot Festus." She pushed up to a sitting position and looked around, her eye's large. "My phone is in his pocket." She nodded toward Louis McKenzie. "He took it from me downstairs."

Oscar pulled his phone from his back pocket and slid it to Fifer. "Call 911," he said, his voice a little more normal sounding. His eyes pulled from Fifer to his dog. "Hold pressure on Festus's wound." The blood drained from Oscar's face, and he looked back at Fifer. "Are you okay? Did he hurt you?"

"I'm okay." Fifer sniffed and turned back to Festus. She looked at the bright red spot on his hip. Festus whimpered and lifted his head. She slid closer to him, cradling the dog's head in her lap as she dialed the number.

"How is he?" Oscar's voice called from behind her.

Fifer's tears fell on the dog. She leaned forward and pressed her palm against the wound. Festus whimpered again, but didn't open his eyes. "I need the police and an ambulance," Fifer yelled into the phone. "Hurry, someone's been shot."

Monday afternoon found Oscar resting his head on the back of his couch. It had been an incredible weekend. After the police and the ambulance arrived at Fifer's house Friday evening, Fifer had insisted the EMTs ignore the people and work on Festus. Oscar smiled at the memory. The medical workers had wanted to protest, but Fifer threatened to do bodily harm to them if they didn't help the animal. It was a sight.

Once Louis McKenzie was in cuffs, Oscar, with Fifer at his side, had scooped up his dog and rushed him across town to the vet. The bullet had gone through the animal's hip, missing the bone by a hair's breadth. Festus stayed at the vet for the rest of the weekend, and Oscar picked him up earlier that afternoon after work. Festus had a shaved spot with stitches that he was not supposed to lick and an antibiotic to take with his food. The vet assured them he would heal up good as new.

Oscar looked over his shoulder from where he sat on his couch, with Festus stretched out next to him, the dog's head in his lap. "It wasn't funny then, but you have to admit, it's pretty funny now."

"They're in the medical field and specifically trained for emergencies." Fifer didn't have to ask what Oscar was talking about. He was not going to let her forget her little show of authority any time soon. "It was an emergency." She walked back from the kitchen with two cups of coffee. She handed one cup to Oscar, then sat in the chair at a right angle to his couch. "Just because I told . . ."

Oscar held up a hand and interrupted her, mirth dripping from his words. "Demanded would be the word I would use here."

"Whatever," Fifer said, rolling her eyes. "I was a little excited, okay? So were you. But just because I *demanded* they check on Festus was no reason for them to get all huffy, like checking on our boy was beneath them or something."

"They were surprised, is all." Oscar sipped his coffee. "I know those men, and they're good people, but they were responding to a gunshot call. When they got there, they found out the victim was my dog." He grinned. "The funny part is, neither one of them had the guts to tell you they didn't work on animals." He leaned forward and set his mug on the coffee table. "You're a sight to behold when you're all worked up like that."

Fifer took a long drink of her coffee. "I don't ever plan on getting that upset again." She reached over and stroked Festus's head. "What did Odi say when you talked to him a while ago? Does it look like they are going to charge my . . . ." She paused and frowned. "That *man* with attempted murder?"

"They've charged him already." Oscar looked at Fifer, biting her lower lip. "Try not to worry. Odi said the police feel they can build a solid case against him. The man drove down here intending to take you back to Birmingham and kill you. They have your testimony, and they've also tracked down Joseph DeCroux. The man you said is his right-hand guy. They put some pressure on him. To save his own neck, the guy admitted that Louis McKenzie told him his plan with all the details."

"What will happen to the dinner theater now?" Fifer pushed her hair back over her shoulder. "I am so ready for this to be over."

"Since they aren't investigating his company, and right now the charges are against him personally, he can sell us his share."

"But will he?" Fifer leaned back in her chair and massaged the muscles in her neck. "He'll hold on to it now just to spite me."

"I don't know." Oscar looked at Fifer. She was exhausted. Even for a person as tough as her, this was a lot to deal with. "Let me and Odi handle it. If we can convince him it's in his best interest to cut ties with our little town, I imagine he'll sign everything over. You may not believe it, but the Robinson men can be pretty persuasive when they need to be."

"I wish you didn't need to be."

"Fifer." Oscar sat forward and took her hand. "This is not your fault. A narcissist decided to use you and punish you for something your mother and your uncle did. You've got to remember that."

"I will." Fifer's thumb rubbed across the top of Oscar's knuckles. "I'm just wondering what other lies he's fed me through the years to keep me under his thumb. I knew he didn't love me. When I was little, I thought it was because I was too loud or not pretty enough or whatever. When I was older, I thought it was because I killed my mother."

"Do you think he was not telling the truth about the accident?"

"Possibly. Probably. I don't know. I was so messed up back

then, so insecure, that I went into rehab without questioning anything. When I came out, it was all over. I wanted to forget it, and I did. I really can't remember much of what happened."

"Is there someone you can contact that can help you find out the facts from that night?" Oscar slid closer to the edge of the couch and Festus moved to keep his head on Oscar's lap. "Someone you trust?"

"Yes. There's a private investigator that helped me find out the little I actually know about Louis McKenzie's history. I'm going to give him a call." She reached over and ran her fingers along Oscar's scruffy jawline. "Just think. For a few sweet hours on Thursday and Friday, we thought things were going our way. Thought we would be married right now."

"Things are going our way, Fifer." Oscar captured her hand in his and kissed her fingertips. "God's hand is in this. Don't doubt it. If we'd just bought your fath—Louis McKenzie—out like we'd planned. He would have always been in your life one way or another. Men like him don't give up and walk away from something they see as theirs. What happened was hard. Is hard." He paused and looked down at Festus. "And innocents had to suffer. But in the long run, we have won. He's going to jail, we will get the dinner theater, and we. Will. Get. Married."

"Promise?"

Oscar squeezed her hand. "You have my word."

Two weeks. That's how long it had taken Oscar and Odi

to get Louis McKenzie to sign over his part of the dinner theater. Fifer wasn't sure how they did it, but she was sure it involved Odi going out of town to Birmingham for a few days. When he came back, McKenzie signed the paperwork without any further backlash from him or his lawyer.

In the meantime, she'd been very busy. She'd uncovered all kinds of interesting facts about what had happened the night her mother died. Now that Louis McKenzie was going down, losing his iron grip on those around him, people were remembering things and talking a lot more freely.

The PI uncovered the name of one of the police officers, as well as the two EMTs, who worked the scene of her crash that night all those years ago. Shortly after the accident, all three men had stepped down from their jobs, the policeman retiring, one EMT opening a deli, the other EMT moving away, then dying of a drug overdose shortly after.

"The EMT that got out of the medical field and opened the deli said you were wandering around outside the vehicle, bleeding everywhere, your arm hanging at a funny angle." The PI sat in the coffee shop and looked across the table at Fifer. The man had graying hair at his temples and a few wrinkles at the corners of his eyes, but looked like he could double as a navy seal. "The other EMT was checking on your mother, who was definitely wedged behind the steering wheel of the car. Before the first EMT could get to you, you hit the ground by the driver's side door nearby and passed out."

"So, my mother was driving the car all along?"

"Yes." The PI slid a folder across the table to Fifer. "From what I have found, there was never any doubt that your mother was driving. Nowhere in here is there any mention of bringing you up on charges of manslaughter." He opened the folder and slid out a few photos. He pointed to the one on top. "This picture clearly shows how the car hit the tree. Your mother was killed instantly. You must have had your seatbelt on, or you would have died too." He pointed to a man standing near an ambulance in the background of another photo. "That is the EMT who died of the drug overdose less than a year after the accident."

Fifer's forehead wrinkled. She studied the photos, trying to remember that night, but nothing came back to her. She finally looked up at the man across the table, staring at her intently. "It is strange that all three men who were first to the scene left their jobs shortly after that."

"Miss McKenzie, your father is a ruthless man. I talked to the EMT and the cop and they both acted scared to death when I mentioned your father's name. The only reason I got what I did was because they heard about your father trying to kill you and that he's in jail. I think he paid off all three of them to make sure that when you did start asking questions, they wouldn't be around to answer them."

"I only asked questions a couple of times, but nobody ever told me anything." Fifer looked closely at the three men in the photos. "I was a scared kid at Louis McKenzie's mercy, but not anymore. Do you think that guy really died of an overdose?" she asked, pointing to one of the EMTs. "Or did my fa—Louis McKenzie—end his life?"

"I don't know, but something is fishy. His mother said her son had never used drugs and didn't believe for a second that he had overdosed." The PI watched Fifer stack up the photos and put them in the folder. "I'm sure I can find out more about this if you want me to. And now that he's in custody, I imagine some of the weaker links in his chain may break as well. Just tell me what you want me to do."

"I'm going to get this and the other things you got me before to my future brother-in-law to make sure the right authorities see it. He assures me Louis McKenzie will go away for life, but I also want them to understand that I have been manipulated through all of this, just like almost everyone else that has dealt with him over the years."

Fifer thanked the man and watched him walk out of the pastry shop. Mr. Bob, the owner of the establishment, who was also one of her AA buddies, stepped from around the counter and walked over to where Fifer sat.

"You've been through a whole lot over the past few weeks, girl." Bob wiped his hands on his black canvas apron and sat in the recently abandoned chair. "How're you holding up?"

"I struggled a little one night." Fifer's eyes looked tenderly at the old man. "But I called Eric. We talked a little while, I did some serious praying, exercised until my tongue was hanging out, and made it through. Other than that, I've held up well. Thank you for being concerned."

"Know that if you ever can't get Eric, you can call me." Bob rubbed his fingers along his cheek, prickly with gray whiskers. "I don't have the words like Eric does, but I will be there for you if you need me."

Fifer blinked back tears. "I don't deserve friends like you and Eric and the Robinsons. You have taken me in and made me one of you."

"That's what we're supposed to do, according to what the Bible says, right? Bear one another's burdens?"

"It is." Fifer pulled a napkin from the holder in the middle of the table and wiped her nose. "But you saw who I was before. I wasn't exactly nice to the people of Red Creek when I first got here."

"But you're not that gal anymore, are you?"

"No. Thank the Lord. I'm not. She's gone. Forever."

Epilogue

Eighteen months later

Oscar pulled a chair out at a corner table away from the stage in the front of the dinner theater and waited for Fifer to sit down. He watched her adjust her loose-fitting dress around her barely noticeable baby bump. He stood behind the chair and looked around the room, filled with the ever-increasing tourist crowd, along with several locals, all waiting for his mother and father to take the stage.

"The usual, Mrs. Robinson?" The young waiter stepped up to the table, and Oscar sat down beside his wife. He watched the teen put a basket of warm chips and a container of salsa on the table between them.

"I think I'll have chicken and shrimp fajitas tonight, Reg," Fifer said, plucking a chip from the basket. "And bring some guacamole for these chips, please. And iced tea for both of us."

Oscar put in his order for the Orville Special, which was two hard-shelled tacos and two soft shelled tacos, one beef and one chicken of each kind, a cheese enchilada, with Spanish rice and refried beans on the side. "I have to admit Momma was right about making this place a Tex-Mex restaurant." He took a chip from the basket and looked around the room. "We get as many locals for the food, I think, as we do tourists for the entertainment."

"Your mother has an amazing sixth sense for this sort of thing. I imagine that's where your brother Owen gets his talent for managing the place."

"Probably so." Oscar stopped and listened as Owen stepped behind the mic on the stage area at the front of the theater. His brother had a touch of showmanship to him as he announced his mother, the famous Nashville one-of-a-kind talent who had returned to her beloved Alabama roots. He next introduced his enormously talented song-writer, Grammy award winning father, who could play almost any instrument he touched. Oscar chuckled as Owen almost tripped and fell into his father as his parents took the stage. Did his brother do that on purpose, or was it his normal clumsiness kicking in? With Owen, you couldn't be sure. Everything Owen just said about their parents was true to a certain extent, but he certainly had a way of making it seem grand. Somehow, the showman gene had passed him, Odi, and Oliver by. Maybe Olivia too, but he wasn't sure about her yet.

"Aw." Fifer jutted her chin toward a gray-haired couple taking the dance floor in front of the theater area as Orville and Lucy began singing "Our Head Strong Love." The guitars, mandolin, drums and banjo in the band blended with Orville on the fiddle. "Let's dance, Oscar. Before I'm so big, all I'll be able to do is waddle."

"I'll waddle right along with you when the time gets here." Oscar stood and held out his hand to Fifer. He looked at the simple engagement ring and wedding band snuggled on the ring finger of her left hand. "You lead, and I'll follow."

Lucy Robinson's Country Dinner Theater had opened six

months ago, only a little behind schedule, almost the exact same time Louis McKenzie had been found guilty of the attempted murder of Fifer. The court gave him forty years without parole, but since that time, they'd also charged him with the deaths of four other people he was associated with over the past twenty years. This did not include the EMT who'd been at Fifer's wreck all those years ago. The police were still looking into that, plus a lot of other crimes that seemed to lead back to Louis McKenzie's doorstep.

Oscar moved slowly in rhythm with the music and Fifer's steps as she snuggled close to him, her head on his shoulder. The dinner theater was doing remarkably well. Orville had asked to buy out both Oscar's and the Crestfield brothers' portion of the establishment.

At first, Oscar wondered if his father had made the offer so Oscar could go ahead in pursuing his own dream of the fishing camp. Now, however, he knew better. Lucy Robinson excelled in show business, and Orville loved having a business that his family actually wanted to be involved in along with him. Oscar hadn't told his father yet, but after the baby was born, he and Fifer planned to sell him their share of the dinner theater as he wanted. What the Crestfields would do was still up in the air, but Oscar knew the men. Bill would eventually need capital for his next big venture, and Grant did whatever Bill decided. Orville just needed to bide his time, and the entire operation would be his. If there was one thing his father was good at, it was waiting for the things he really wanted to come about.

After the song finished, Oscar and Fifer returned to their seats. "Married life looks good on you, Fifer Robinson." Oscar watched his wife scoop piping hot onions, peppers, meats, and the other fixings into her tortilla. "I do believe you're the most beautiful woman in this place."

"And I do believe you are full of it." Fifer slathered a layer of guacamole and sour cream on the tortilla, then raised it to her lips. "But I love you, anyway." She took a bite of her food and sighed. "Festus would love this. Let's order him a doggy bag."

"That dog has put on ten pounds since you got pregnant." Oscar reached over and wiped a dribble of sour cream from Fifer's chin. They had married six months after her father broke into her house. Fifer had insisted they wait until she was sure she would not be brought up on any charges related to her father's business before she would marry Oscar. "I don't want to have my husband come visit me in the slammer," she had said, every time he tried to get her to change her mind.

The DA finally assured her everyone knew she was an innocent victim of Louis McKenzie's schemes, and no manslaughter charges were hanging over her head related to her mother's death. She and Oscar had celebrated by going to the justice of the peace that Wednesday morning and tying the knot.

"What's that?" Fifer's eyes narrowed as Odi walked up with a long cardboard tube and sat down beside Oscar.

"Hello to you too, sister-in-law," Odi said, passing the tube to Oscar. He reached into the chip basket and helped himself to a warm chip. "Ask your husband. I'm just the delivery guy."

"Well?" Fifer looked at Oscar, one eyebrow raised. "Is it something good?"

"I think so." Oscar tapped the tube against the palm of his hand. "But I like log cabins. If you don't like log cabins, we may need to chuck these house plans and start over."

"House plans." Fifer lowered her fork back to her plate. "For us?"

"And Festus. And Festus, Junior."

"We are not naming our baby Festus, junior, but Oscar . . ." Fifer leaned forward and kissed Oscar on the lips. "I love a log cabin. Especially if I can look out my front door and see a creek bank."

"Then you are going to love this one, Fifer Robinson. And I love you."

Continue reading for a sneak peek at Our Unlikely Love, book three in the Red Creek Redemption series.

Our Unlikely Love

"Aww man." Owen Robinson looked down at the blob of grape jelly on his crisp white button-down shirt. "Not another one. I'll have to change before the meeting now."

"Why don't you just wear a bib and be done with it?" Olivia, Owen's youngest sibling and only sister, sat across from him. Her twin brother Oliver completed the family trio at the breakfast table of her loft apartment above her restaurant. "I bet your cleaning bill is higher than mine and Oliver's put together."

"No." Owen reached down and swiped his finger across the jelly, lifting the excess and sticking it in his mouth, but rubbing the residue thoroughly into the white cotton fabric. "I've tried the cleaners a few times, and it's hit and miss. I don't bother with it much anymore."

"What do you mean you don't bother with it?" Olivia quit buttering her twice toasted biscuit, a favorite of her brothers. She always had fresh biscuits on her menu downstairs. If there were a few left over at the end of the day, she would pop them open the next morning, butter and toast them for breakfast.

Owen and Oliver were sure to visit if she texted and let them know what was on her morning table. "Please don't tell me you're throwing away that shirt."

"Of course not." Owen picked up a piece of bacon from his plate and bit the end off. "I'm not made of money like you and the rest of the family." He winked at Olivia and she poked her lips out like a duck. "I donate my stained shirts to Sheltered Arms. That way, when they sell them, the money goes to help the food bank and the homeless shelters."

"That's good." Oliver took a drink of his milk. "That place helps a lot of folks."

"Good, yeah." Olivia poked her butter knife in Owen's direction. "But it's still wasteful on your part. If you would go ahead and treat that stain now, before it sets, your shirt would be good as new. But you'll leave it in your truck or on your floor for a couple of weeks before you even attempt to do anything with it."

Oliver looked from his little sister, younger by two minutes, to his older brother and grinned. Watching the two spar was more entertaining than anything he could find on TV or the internet.

"I don't have time for all that domestic stuff." Owen picked up his coffee and took a long sip. "I work, remember."

"Duh." Olivia gave Owen an exaggerated blink of her gray eyes, similar to his except Owen's were fringed in naturally thick, coal black lashes that any woman would die for. "Who do you think runs this place? And"—she drug the word out slowly. "Who fixes your breakfast at least three times a week to make sure you don't starve to death?"

"You love doing this kind of stuff, though." Owen set down his mug. "I think it comes natural to you to clean and cook and take care of people."

Oliver's eyes darted from Owen to his sister, like he was watching a Wimbledon tennis match. Olivia's biscuit stopped halfway between her saucer and her lips. "Owen Robinson, if you weren't my brother, I'd box your ears. I do enjoy cooking and feeding you and the rest of the family, but it's a ton of hard work to keep a restaurant going, much less be a wife and mother on top of that." She set the biscuit down on her plate and leaned forward, a twinkle growing in her eye. "You know what you need?"

Owen's eyebrows raised slowly and a bit of skepticism with a smidge of fear entered his tone. "What?" He'd seen that look on his sister's face before. It never ended well.

"You need a woman."

Owen glanced at Oliver, his head suddenly bowed like he was praying, but his shoulders were suspiciously shaking. "I hope you mean a maid, because I already know that. I just haven't gotten around to trying to find somebody yet."

"That's not what I mean, and you know it." Olivia picked her biscuit back up and tore off a bite. "You need a maid too, don't get me wrong. You could almost pay the woman's salary in the amount you spend on new shirts."

"You're probably right." Owen sighed. "Do you know anybody that would do a good job and not try to change my stuff around? I hate people meddling in my stuff."

"Let me think on it." Olivia smiled. "I bet I can find you somebody."

Oliver wiped the napkin across his lips and stood. "Breakfast was great, sis. Thanks again. I've got to run. I've got hall duty at school this morning."

Owen glanced at his watch. "I've got to go too." He pushed his chair back and stood, grabbing the back of the chair before it tumbled over. "Tell Quinn to give me a call if he wants to go squirrel hunting this weekend with me and Mr. Blue."

"Hmmm?" Olivia looked up and blinked, her thoughts still on Owen's love life— or lack of one.

"Squirrel hunting?" Owen reached down and picked up his coffee cup and gulped down the last swallow. He snapped his fingers in front of her face. "This weekend? Tell Quinn?"

"Yeah, yeah." Olivia nodded slowly, finally blinking out of her matchmaking thoughts. "I'll tell him."

Owen shrugged, set the mug down and hurried after Oliver, who was already going out the back door and down the stairs to the parking lot behind the restaurant. "Wait up, Oli."

Oliver, the quietest member of the Robinson clan, turned as he reached his truck. His lips turned up at the corners. "You know what she's gonna do, right?"

"Who?"

"Olivia." Oliver hit the button on his truck fob. "I'm glad it's you and not me."

"What?" Owen's brow wrinkled. "Who?" He ran his fingers through his dark brown hair, not as black as his father's, but not as light as the twins. He looked at Oliver. "What did I miss this time?"

"Olivia." Oliver slapped Owen on the back. "Didn't you see that look on her face? You just became her new project." He looked at Owen's blank expression and snorted. "You really do live in your own little world sometimes, brother. She's going to find you a woman, Owen. You practically invited her to stick her nose into your love life."

"Me?" Owen's eyes narrowed, trying to recall what he'd said to give Oliver this impression. He'd always had a little trouble paying attention. Thoughts tended to jump through his brain like he was flipping stations on a radio. A lot of the time, if he didn't make a special effort to focus, he changed the station too soon and missed half of what was being said around him. Most of the time, through years of practice, he still heard everything and could pull it back up later and sort out the details if he tried hard enough. What had he missed a few minutes ago that made Olivia want to be his matchmaker? "She's going to help me find a cleaning lady."

"Think, brother." Oliver stepped back and opened his truck door. "This is Olivia you're talking about. The sister who has been in your business since she was big enough to say your name. She's mothered you ever since she was in diapers."

Owen watched his brother get into his truck. Oliver was right. Other than her twin, Olivia was probably closer to him than she was to any of the other Robinsons. Oscar, the oldest Robinson, older than Owen by less than two years, had taken on the role of second father to the siblings. He'd often been stern as a kid, mimicking their father's behavior and distancing himself from the rest of the rowdy brood like a miniature adult. Olivia and Oliver, a little over three years younger than Owen, had been his own personal toys growing up.

Any crazy scheme he'd dreamed up as a kid, he'd always brought the two younger siblings, especially dare-devil Olivia, into. When he'd swiped his father's lighter, back when he was nine and the twins were six, and nearly set the woods on fire, Olivia had been right there beside him, watching the blaze. Oliver, the child with a good dose of common sense, had run to the garden on the other side of the house to get their father to come and put out the growing inferno. That was the year their father quit smoking.

Six months later, when Owen set the woods on fire again with a magnifying glass and a milk jug, Olivia had been amazed—Orville Robinson—not so much. "Son, if these woods blaze again, I don't care if the Almighty sets them on fire with lightning. I'm going to whip you into next week. Your cheeks are going to burn way worse than those pine trees you torched." Owen had learned to control his curiosity related to pyrotechnics after that. He'd also prayed hard every time it rained for the next year, begging God to keep the lightning in the sky and not let it touch down anywhere near his house.

Owen raised his hand and saluted Oliver as he drove away, still thinking about the conversation at the breakfast table. Owen was sure Oliver was correct. His quiet brother could read most people like a book, but especially Olivia. If Oliver said their sister had gone into matchmaking mode, then Owen might as well write it down. She'd be calling him soon to set him up on some kind of date.

He stepped over to his truck and looked at the mud caked down the side. It had rained several days last week and made the woods behind his father's house perfect for riding his four-wheeler. He'd spent hours Saturday slinging up mud with his ATV, jumping gullies, running through ditches filled with slime and water, and making a mess in general. When he was done, he'd tossed his mud-caked jeans and the rest of his clothes in the back of the truck where they still were, then went skinny-dipping in Red Creek. He'd driven home in some gym shorts he found behind the truck seat with intentions of washing his truck Sunday after church. He'd hosed off the four-wheeler that afternoon but received a phone call from Mr. Blue and got distracted before the rest of the job got done.

He climbed into his filthy truck and turned toward Red Creek. He had to be at the Blue Hotel in a while, but he had time to run through town. He still worked for Mr. Blue part-time, even though his main job now was helping his parents manage the dinner theater they'd opened earlier in the year. If he hurried, he could run through the car wash before he went home to change his shirt. The car wash would kill two birds with one stone. The jeans still in the truck bed were one of his best pair. He'd been on the phone with his mother and forgotten to change into older ones on Saturday when he decided to go mud riding on the four-wheeler. If they didn't come clean in the car wash, then he'd take them to Sheltering Arms with his pile of shirts.

Olivia was right about one thing. He spent entirely too much money on clothes. He had to look nice at work. It was an expected part of his job. At the Blue Hotel, he was required to wear the white oxford cloth shirts with a tie and dress pants. He kept a sports coat handy there as well, in case Mr. Blue had a group or special function going on and needed him to look more professional. At his parent's place, the attire was nice, high-dollar jeans, like the ones in his truck bed, a button-up or western shirt, and cowboy boots. He had a hat too but didn't wear it often because he kept forgetting where he left it. Having a woman around to clean, pick up after him, organize his schedule—yes, that would be amazing. Well, as long as she didn't get into his business. That's the thing that blew his mind about his parents, Olivia and her husband Quinn, and now his big brother Oscar and his wife Fifer . . . especially Oscar and Fifer. They were always in each other's business, like it didn't bother them at all. Like it was expected, like they enjoyed being attached at the hip.

He didn't get it. What would a girlfriend think about mud riding just for the fun of it? Sliding around in the muck, slinging it to kingdom come, being covered from head to toe where only the whites of his eyes showed. It was sort of freeing. And skinny dipping, that was the same thing, but different at the same time. His mind reveled in the craziness of it and he wasn't hurting anyone. No, a girlfriend would probably tell him he needed to grow up. Why? He paid his bills. He worked hard.

Owen pulled his truck up to the automated car wash and paid at the kiosk for the top-level deal. The lady at the entrance waved him onto the conveyor, motioning for him to turn his tires to the left, then to put it in neutral. She gave him a wink and a thumbs up as his truck crept by into the tunnel, the thick foam plopping on his hood followed by the beating of the water from the high-powered sprayers. No, as long as he could do his life his way, stained shirts and muddy truck included, he would continue to fly solo. Olivia would have to get over it.

If you enjoyed Oscar and Fifer's story, please consider leaving a review.

Thoughts About The Story

Our Unfailing Love was a very hard book for me to write. As a matter of fact, when I started writing *Family Smarts and Runaway Hearts*, I discovered at about chapter ten that my heroine had a secret drinking problem. This heroine, named Honey, was not someone I wanted to write about. So, I tossed that book in the *did not finish* pile and wrote the current book that is published with the same name. Olivia replaced Honey as my heroine and brought her own set of problems that were not as close to home for me and were easier to write about.

Then two books later, when I started writing about Fifer, guess what started sneaking into the story? After a lot of prayer and whining about not wanting to tackle this subject, I finally sat back down at my keyboard and wrote *Our Unfailing Love*.

I grew up with alcoholism in my family. Not my mother or father, but a grandfather and a sibling. I didn't know my grandfather. He died before I was born. But my dear brother struggled with his addiction until the day he died. He was one of the sweetest souls I've ever known and he hated his monster with a passion. He would break free for long periods of time, but it always found a way to return and lure him in.

This brother was the one who got me to read my Bible from cover to cover. He knew God was his only hope of redemption for this sin and all the others we get tangled up in. I have mine, you have yours. Just like Lucy Robinson said, some folks' sins are easier to see than others.

I know my brother is in heaven now with a new body. His new body will never have to deal with alcohol or its horrible consequences. I look forward to seeing him one day without his monster snapping at his heels. Thank God for redemption.

A Little About KC

KC sincerely believes that well-written Christian fiction can change lives. When a novel has strong Christian principals woven intricately into a well-written plot, the reader bonds with lifelike characters who struggle with trials, temptations, and struggles that the reader identifies with. The reader identifies with these characters because she's been there. Everyone has fallen. That's why everyone needs a Savior.

Then, when these same characters turn to Christ the Savior to bring them through these dark moments, the reader finds hope. KC believes the story reminds the reader why she must lean on the Lord in her trying situations. Through the book's structure showing Christianity as the positive light for good that KC knows to be true, the reader also sees why she needs to be the hands and feet of Christ to others.

KC strives to show how the Lord uses situations, people, and His Word to bring the lost to Him, and mold, prune and grow His children. She tackles challenging situations, powerful emotions, and spiritual warfare through engaging stories and true-to-life characters.

KC's favorite Bible verses are Philippians 2:5-8. Have this mind among yourselves, which is yours in Christ Jesus, who, though he was in the form of God, did not count equality with God a thing to be grasped, but made himself nothing, taking the form of a servant, being born in the likeness of men. And being found in human form, he humbled himself by becoming obedient to the point of death, even death on a cross.

KC cannot read these words without getting a lump in her throat. She strives daily to use her writing, her platform, her small influence to show others the love Christ has shown her.

If you enjoyed this book, please take a few minutes to leave a review. Authors, myself included, really appreciate this, and it helps draw more readers to books they may enjoy as well. A few words are appreciated.
Thanks! KC

Join KC's newsletter and receive a free ebook of Music Smarts and Humble Hearts

Follow KC on her social media platforms

https://www.goodreads.com/author/show/20570083.
K_C_Hart

https://www.bookbub.com/profile/kc-hart?list=
author_books

https://www.facebook.com/KCWRITESBOOKS

Also By
KC Hart

Our Head Strong Love
A Christmas Blaze
Fresh Starts and Small Town Hearts
Business Smarts and Reckless Hearts
Car Smarts and Bashful Hearts
People Smarts and Wounded Hearts
Kid Smarts and Wistful Hearts
Family Smarts and Runaway Hearts
Elsie: Prairie Roses Collection
Moonlight, Murder and Small Town Secrets
Music, Murder and Small Town Romance
Memories. Murder and Small Town Money
Merry Murder and Small Town Santas
Medicine Murder and Small Town Scandal
Marriage, Murder & Small Town Schemes
Mistaken Murder & Small Town Status
Mistletoe, Murder & Small Town Scoundrels

Join KC's newsletter and receive a free ebook of Music Smarts and
Humble Hearts

If you enjoy my books, please consider leaving a review where you purchased them. Reviews help an author in so many ways.

Blessings,

KC Hart

The Katy Cross Cozy Mystery Series

The Carson's Bayou Romance Series

Fresh Starts and Small Town Hearts

Business Smarts and Reckless Hearts

Car Smarts and Bashful Hearts

People Smarts and Wounded Hearts

Kid Smarts and Wistful Hearts

Family Smarts and Runaway Hearts

Music Smarts and Humble Hearts
(Only available through newsletter
subscription)

The Red Creek Redemption Romance Series

Our Head Strong Love

Our Unfailing Love